The Guest Informant

David Stokes

To the beautiful Camilla
from your friend

[signature]

 New Generation **Publishing**

Chapter 1

At first it sounded like the sea screaming. The yells and screams were so inhuman, so unexpected. A few seconds later it sounded like gulls. Then the first impression returned, in the absence of other living beings. Standing under the influence of the lighthouse, convinced the sea is screaming.

Slipping back into Aristotelian logic I reassure my mind that the sea is inanimate and that the inanimate does not scream. Hence the sea is not screaming. Reassured I pace out about twenty yards to a point overlooking the bay. In the distance four teenagers are larking on the strand. Two boys, two girls. It's the girls yelling and screaming; not the sea.

From the very first night I was at the mercy of the cosmos and the sea, the stars like mystical illuminations in the darkness of infinity. It's impossible to comprehend their beauty as a chemical process of helium and hydrogen. Here cities are tangential, civilization unimportant. The only meaningful use of time is remembering ancient Norse and Greek names for star-gods.

I turn from the vantage point overlooking the bay, thinking that Sonia would have been about their age, even though she looked and acted much older. When a human being takes the life of another human being they step outside the ordinary parameters of human responsibility and into a universal role. Sooner or later that becomes apparent, even if it takes decades. On the short walk to the cottage I try to imagine the kind of life Sonia might have had. Then in a moment of near-panic I put that right out of my mind. The sanctuary of the sea is not even enough to hold that thought in place for longer than a second or two.

I'd searched the East coast of Ireland in a hire-car until I found the cottage. I fidgeted with the car-keys as the auctioneer explained the rental details, trying not to show how desperately I needed to close the deal. I re-assured Corinne by text-message and during brief, uneasy phone-conversations, explaining in various ways why I had to get out of London. But she didn't understand. It all happened so quickly, the nausea and dizziness near rail-tracks and underground stations. It had got to where just the sight of a London underground station brought on panic.

I haven't slept apart from Corinne for over twenty years and life without her is meaningless. I understand she couldn't have just dropped everything to come with me. She doesn't think it's that serious, thinks I'll snap out of it. But I'm not snapping out of it. For hours at a time the fear of losing her dominates all other emotions, the fear that no other woman would take me on if she left. The fear too that she doesn't love me as much as she used to. When an ordinary man's emotional life is jigsawed together by a woman she has the power of life and death over him. He's gifted her his independence, his reason for living in the world. If this can't be sorted out, or if in sorting it out I lose Corinne, then it is pointless going on. There'd be no way of surviving her loss. No way of stumbling through whatever days remain without her as a guide.

There'd been little time to pack and the cottage looks as bare as if it's still unoccupied. A frayed and broken-spined edition of 'The Encyclopedia of Chess Openings' rests by a chess-board with the pieces arranged as per the culmination of the Korchoi-Karpov match in 1978. I'm again absorbed in that world championship match, digging out thirty year old yellowing newspaper cuttings that I'd brought from where they were buried in a dusty drawer in our house in Greenford. The analysis of the games by the chess newspaper' correspondents excavate forgotten meanings. On the first night here I stared at the newspaper cuttings and then at the lighthouse as it beamed majestic signals to cargoes on the Irish Sea. Waiting, murmuring prayers to gods I don't believe in, waiting for the revelation to come.

The vulgar bungalow just on the other side of the lighthouse peninsula is the only habitation for miles. A t.v satellite dish is bolted to its exterior like armour against the natural beauty of the coast. From the very first hours on the coast I sensed eyes were watching from that bungalow. Shadows fading as they stepped backwards away from the window. On the margin of one of the newspaper cuttings from the Korchnoi-Karpov match there's a tight pattern of inked sentences. The ink hasn't faded, the words of the French murderer Leconte as readable as when they were first written. 'If one has to think about one's victims, one wouldn't be able to go on living.' It's definitely my handwriting. And I'd signed it too. Scrawled the place and year under my name. 'Brussels 1978'.

The headaches and dizziness are passing, now that there's nothing straight ahead only the view of the peninsula and the lighthouse through the back-window of the cottage. Lights wink in the darkness of the bay - the power-boats of cannabis-smugglers or trawlers chugging towards Carnsore. The views are a truth-serum for the memory, shortening the distance between the reality of the coast and the moments in the past I know I have to plunder.

Corinne's look when I said I had to leave London for a while follows me to the coast, forming the last conscious image in my thoughts on the coastal nights to come. She's busy with her school's yearly inspection so I can't get through to her in the working hours. And she's retiring to bed earlier and earlier, so it's hell trying to get through to her at all. When I place the contract phone I brought with me from London on the table it becomes a synthesis of everything of meaning in life.

On the first night I propped the divan against one wall of the cottage back-room, where the window faces the sea. From the back-room the lighthouse is visible so that's where I sleep, ignoring the bedroom at the front of the cottage. At night my thoughts are darkened by fears about murder detectives from the Belgium police. As I lie sleepless I wonder if they ever lose sleep over unsolved murders from the Brussels of 1978. In the darkness paranoia plays stalking games with a thousand forms of fear.

I'd driven onto the peninsula in a low mood, hopes fading of finding somewhere to rent close to the sea on that first day, reconciling myself to the compromise of a guesthouse or a hotel on the outskirts of a town. The 'to-let' sign outside the cottage by the lighthouse turned the mood of the day upside down. The auctioneer answered straightaway when I rang the number from the to-let sign. He sounded pleased to hear from me, keen to show me the interior. He said it'd take him about an hour to make it to the peninsula. It was a nudge from destiny, the very first moment the lighthouse cottage came into view.

Waiting for the auctioneer I tried to read the coastline by looking at what the sea has washed onto the strand. In the freedom of sea-air, through shingles sprinkled with crab-shells and goose-barnacles, I noticed the delicate white spirula coils lying on the rocks. A child's dolly, naked and caked with mud washed up among the calcite skeletons of sea-urchins and cuttlefish. And further on. Close to the lighthouse, the husk of a rotted lobster-pot bobbed among sargassum seaweed and plastic soda bottles.

A purple sandpiper preened in the headland. Grebes and warblers skimmed stony beaches in the direction of the brackish mires of the sloblands further up the coast. Just off the peninsula terns from Lady's Island were passing. The sea worked a spell, chasing off the worse of the fears that followed me from London. During the first minutes on the peninsula I wished Corinne was beside me, so as we could set out together to walk through the birds-foot and sea-pen plants in the dunes and mudflats. Mesmerised by the birdlife, touched by the sea.

The auctioneer was surprised that I wanted the keys straightaway, before he'd a chance to make the cottage habitable. But the man means nothing to me, as I mean nothing to him. So it doesn't matter if he noticed my desperation.

In the cottage the remaining daylight hours pass quickly. The kids larking on the strand are forgotten, their world at an immeasurable point from this interior. In the dark with the beams from the lighthouse hypnotising the bay, everything about my life in London is abstract and unnecessary. Regrets from the years before I'd even met Corinne drag bloodied feet past the reviewing stand of memory, the same names hung out in the same high winds of conscience. If I hadn't met Marco all those years ago how differently it all might have worked out. In the back-room of the cottage, facing the lighthouse I reflect on my apprenticeship for the first time in an age. Spectral images of my father form on the window-panes, a lifetime's disappointment worked into the lines on his forehead.

That look on my father's face as he handed me M. Goudron's acceptance letter for the final year of my apprenticeship was the beginning of the journey that ended in the attic rooms of the Hotel Eugene Plasky. A goldsmith's apprenticeship back then spanned a full seven years with a further five years of finishing work. They taught us how to set, micro-set, design, mount, polish and enamel. And then as part of an exchange scheme they sent me to Belgium to complete my papers as a qualified goldsmith. As I'm caught up in the past, wondering how everything went wrong, the phone rings.

I fumble stupidly with the handset, caught up in a mania, hoping its Corinne even though it's almost midnight.

Corinne ... I thought you'd be asleep.

How can I sleep?

Sorry ... that all this is happening.

John ... I've been thinking about everything you said. It's obvious you're having a nervous breakdown.

Her voice tails off, probably tears falling too. I can't just blurt out the truth, let the one woman in the world who loves me know what a monster she's been living with. Her voice steadies when she says the cats are missing me, particularly my favourite of the two. That's what we speak about, the trivia of our intimacy. The school review is weighting on her; that's obvious by the strain in her words when she refers to it. Only after a few minutes she's arrived at a void, too upset to speak any further. I struggle with my own emotions, try to re-assure her that everything will work out okay, that after an appropriate break I'll make it back to Greenford. I miss you, I say conscious that my voice is breaking. Just as I tell her I love her and that I'll see her very soon the phone goes dead. Her tears stay with me all night and into the morning. Men spend entire lifetimes looking for women like Corinne and then a man like me treats her like that. I disgust myself, hate myself for leaving London without her. But I know there wasn't any choice.

In the seascape a grey blur in the darkness marks the beginning of dawn and I wonder if that's enough punishment, to be apart from Corinne for a full day and night. There's so much to contemplate, to begin with, the death of a human being. So this must only be the beginning. Finally in the grey dawn I succumb to sleep. In all our years together we've never had anything like this. There were the expected tensions when we first lived together, but that's a long time ago. We dovetailed perfectly into each other's lives, sharing our wounds each night before sleeping in each other's warmth. I've told her almost everything about my life, except the reason I've abandoned London so abruptly. The things a man can't share with his wife have brought me here.

When I wake on the divan in the back-room of the cottage I instinctively reach out to Corinne. But of course she's in Greenford, reaching out to the empty space in the bed I've left behind. The shock of waking up without her dominates the morning, creates more shadows to stumble through. Out the back-window of the cottage I spot what might be a sea-eagle off the peninsula and the sighting orientates me. It's a startling realisation for one so conditioned by city life. Nothing is so immensely obvious. This must be the sea.

On the radio there's a four metre tide warning but the weather looks calm. Just a short distance from the cottage there's a sloop in dry-dock by an old jetty wall of rotting bricks. The sloop's paintwork is stunning in scarlet and white. From a point on a coastal trail of hardened mud, on a clear day, a field of silver windmills is visible inland. On the shingles I step on the trailing tendrils of a mermaid's purse, emptied of the dogfish eggs it incubated; forlorn by the sea, its duty done. I can only think about Corinne, about how her inspection is going and if she's thinking about me too. There's nothing on the phone, no missed calls or text-messages.

The sea consumes thoughts of Corinne, the sea heaving with renewal like the source of the world's baptismal water. If there are any answers they must be here. Or hope, or reason to go on.

Chapter 2

There's a stooping man waving from a distance off. He's shouting too, like how people shout at dogs straying into danger. I pause on the strand, looking his direction. It's a ploughboy's stoop, probably handed down through his father. There's nobody else around so he must have a reason to speak with me. He jogs the final hundred yards or so, wearing the modern uniform of jeans and sports' top. The sandy hair is a mess. That's apparent from a long way off. He must have it trimmed by an amateur, perhaps a family member with a tendency to hurry. He's somewhere near forty, but it's hard to tell around here; heavier than he needs to be.

I'm Pat Finch, he says breathlessly.

He's holding out a friendly hand. An excessive gesture but I smile anyhow as I take his grip.

I'm John Long. I've just moved into the lighthouse cottage.

I know who you are, he says happily. That's my bungalow just beside you.

He's excited to see the cottage occupied again, sweeping his arm in the direction of the sea as if living in the bungalow naturally entails a custodial role of all one can survey.

I've only rented it for three months. That's the shortest stretch the auctioneer said he can accept.

It doesn't seem to have registered with Pat Finch how limited my time on the coast is, enthusiastic as he is about having a neighbour again.

If you're interested in dogfish or conger eel you've come to the right place, he says pointing towards the rocks by the peninsula. With lugworm on a single hook I've had more than one man's luck. Even at this time 'a the year you can spin for bass off those rocks.

Fishing is not my thing."

He looks at me for a moment as if I've said something totally unexpected. Rubbing his hands together, excited by fishing memories. He alternates hands for the allergic's salute, brushing his nose with a sniff.

I understand, he says sighing. I haven't had time to fish for years. Anyhow the sea from here to the Welsh coast has lost most of its cod. Overfished. It's a wonder there's anything left.

We walk slowly along the promontory in the direction of the lighthouse, easily falling into step with each other.

A thousand ships floundered just over beyond, he says, nodding to a point at the head of the peninsula. Mistook the lighthouse for the light at the Plymouth Sound. Turned aft onto the reefs.

He's proud of the sea, protective of its moods. Not overly intrusive as to the lives of strangers as people might expect him to be. I feel I ought to offer an explanation as to why I'm here anyhow.

13

My wife will be joining me soon ... when she's free from her work.

He takes that information seriously, chewing it over as if trying to fully grasp a life where work separates a man from his woman. He mentions his wife and children, curious about the absence of a vehicle. Cars are legs around here, he says. No car, no legs.

I explain how I hired a car to get here. But that I've no need for it presently; that I plan to explore the peninsula by foot. We walk on silently for some moments in the pallid light of a low-clouded day. The sea-winds are so intoxicating there's no need for unnecessary words. The cries of the seagulls are magnified by the intense quietness of the coast.

Mercury is at its inferior conjunction this evening at nine, he says as we approach the lighthouse.

There's a silence of expectation after he speaks, another moment of surprise. I'm not so burdened by my own troubles that I can't see he's looking for encouragement. I feign interest - offer the chance he's been looking for to talk about the stars.

I've been studying the stars for so long that I'm on intimate terms with them. This winter Mars is in the constellation of Leo. The smallest telescope is enough to make out the dark markings on the surface and the white polar caps.

What's more interesting than Pat Finch's love of cosmology is the look in his eyes. It's a look that everyone in the uglier streets of London knows well but is not what you'd expect to see on the Wexford coast. Pat Finch is lonely, despite everything, the love of wife and children, despite the community he's part of. It's a look I've noticed countless times in London, on tube-trains and at business meetings. In the windows of fast-food restaurants and buses too, when strangers are caught up in everyday kind of fears.

He's wondering what question to ask next. The manual element to his work at a recycling plant is apparent by the smell of industrial cleaning gel, stubby fingers stained by other people's waste. But yet his nights are dedicated to the stars, on the mystery of the cosmos.

There isn't time to listen to a neighbour's obsession with the night-skies. Maybe if we'd met under different conditions, with our wives on holiday. I hand him a tissue for his nose from a pack I keep in my pocket. He wants to keep talking but I've already turned for the cottage. I must find solitude, must isolate an event from the past before it's too late. He calls after me as I go, another observation to do with the stars. But I don't hear the sequence in his words, only the individual words pieced together as a sound. My eyes are on the ground, my thoughts decades away.

Back at the cottage I scatter newspaper cuttings of the Korchnoi-Karpov match on the kitchen table. After so many years the definitive moves of the defector Korchnoi are again just as important as before. Those games in Baguio City, the returning obsession. As an apprentice I followed the opening moves through television and newspapers, lost in the useless thoughts of an unformed man.

Karpov played with the incisiveness of Fischer, the fluidity of play of the Cuban phenomena Capablanca. From the opening game he pressed on Korchnoi, that true master of defence forever harassed by time.

They wonder how murderers can live with themselves. But most human beings live more than one life. The life of the unformed man at twenty or twenty one is not the life of that same man twenty or thirty years later. That's why it's possible to live with oneself, why it's possible to forgive oneself. It's merely an acknowledgment of two lives, not one.

The exchange scheme meant an escape from the deadbeat Sundays of Dublin, the holy hours and the heaving taste of regurgitated porter. Only once in a lifetime. Such things back then didn't happen to people from insignificant Irish midland towns, but yet it happened. I ought to have been more suspicious than what I was. I didn't appreciate the depths of my inadequacies. People rarely do, until they have time to analysis the disasters in their life.

I read the accounts at the time as to how Korchnoi complained about the lightness of the chess pieces, as if it all happened yesterday or the day before. After the Manila magnate Manual Zamora made the necessary phone-calls a heavier set was despatched from Manila over one hundred and fifty miles of rutted mountain road. It arrived fifteen minutes before the scheduled start of play.

The words of the killer Leconte are as potent as when I first copied them in the margin of a newspaper clipping over thirty years ago. The past has arrived within the present, pressing on the passing minutes. The lighthouse cottage contains the rudiments of survival, electricity, doors and windows that lock and unlock adequately. The water in the shower is hot and whoever lived here before left behind a two-band radio with an a.c connection.

I prowl the cottage, organising the few belongings I've brought, listening to a radio talkshow. The radio show callers are angry. They refer to legal writs, raise voices when the radio presenter asks the wrong question. I wonder what happened to the dogma and conventions of my boyhood, the old order of things.

The view from the back-window is distracting me from the reason I came here. I move to the table where the mementos of the Korchnoi-Karpov match roll out an internal screen where again I can see the Goudron studio in Brussels; just how it looked to a twenty two year old out of Dublin for the first time. I'd arrived earlier than they'd expected, planning to find a hotel for a few days before the studio found me the appropriate accommodation for an apprentice.

In the lighthouse cottage street-names form in my mind for the first time in decades; Avenue Fonsny, Rue d'angleterre and Rue Fontaines. Walking the hot summer pavements in the Horta district of Brussels. Stopping every thirty or forty yards to rest the unnecessarily heavy suitcase on the cobbles. At a crepe stall just off Avenue Porte de Hal I paused to look around. Nobody looked back at me. Nobody cared if I lived or died. Nobody estimated my opportunities in life based on the social status of my parents. People freely walked by churches without making brief, frantic gestures meant to symbolise the cross. It was as significant as losing one's virginity or finding a first job, that first experience of true freedom.

The letter-box opens and closes with a disproportionate bang for a simple device. It's a solitary postcard, slotted home in a rush by an unseen hand, addressed to a previous occupant. The panoramic on the front is of a gaudy beach where the palm trees look plastic. I turn it over to read the scrawl of greeting, a little guilty at reading a sentiment intended for someone else. I'm touched by the statement of friendship, even though it's tangential. The day is brightening bravely so I make for the headland; a vague, painful memory of Brussels following me through the door but disintegrating in the awesome presence of the sea. In the headland the yellow of evening primrose and the bunched white of blackthorn look vulnerable against the harsher colours of sea and rock. On the shaper rocks the eyes have been plucked out cleanly from the carcass of an otter, its jaws clamped in posthumous rage. Seals are too far along the peninsula to study without binoculars, their heads visible as they break the water.

Breathless from the hike over heavy ground I make it to a sandy hillock, overcome by the magnitude of the sea. Life in cities appears insane compared to this proximity to the sea. In Brussels I was a man-child of staggering innocence. The Ireland of that time specialised in turning out such freaks. With the exactitude of an interloper I probed the streets of Horta looking for a cheap hotel. Despite the presence of the sea that street from another time is forming in my mind. But then someone shouts from further along the coastal trail. I look around to see a man waving.

It's the man from earlier in the day, Pat Finch from the bungalow. We've only just met but here he is again, looking as if our futures are conjoined. There's no reason for him to come looking for me so soon after we've spoken. Something must have come up. An accident perhaps, or an important piece of local information he forgot to tell me about. He leaves the coastal trail to wade through grass thigh-high in places. He waves again, lifting his legs more purposely in the high grass. He's shouting out his words from several yards off. I don't know where my manners are, he says. I forgot to invite you around for dinner. Or a drink or two at least. The wife would be delighted.

I wonder if there's something wrong with him, if perhaps he's taken alcohol on top of medication. Why can't he see what he's dealing with? He's been looking at me slyly from darkened windows, spoken with me already and the day is only halfway spent. With certain people you have to spell it out. The burden on his soul is hardly my fault, nor the loneliness that's so fundamentally a part of him.

Thanks. Another time perhaps.

Of course. But if you need any help ...

The sea-winds disperse giddily through the headland ferns. If only Corinne was here, if only she'd have put her life on hold. We'd sacrifice entire days and nights to the glory of the sea. The auctioneer smelled vulnerability the second I set foot in his office. When I said I wanted to rent the cottage for a month without blinking he said the minimum rental period is three months. As a connoisseur of human nature, he knew I wouldn't hesitate.

Pat Finch stares at the ground, moving his feet restlessly. I tell him I've somewhere to go and then turn in the direction of the cottage. Predictably he turns that way too, mentioning the sighting of a hump-backed whale further along the coast. He's faltering in his sentences, like a man sent out by his wife or by a parental voice within the structures of his mind to welcome me to the coast. He'd never survive in a big city with such a measure of vulnerability. The closeness of his bungalow to the lighthouse cottage must entail a measure of contact. That's unavoidable. But his need is his own concern. He's not the one who so recently stood on a train platform contemplating a final jump.

He opens his mouth to say something but I raise one hand in the briefest gesture, indicating the cottage. He can see by my expression that I haven't time to hear about Mars in the constellation of Leo or the rate that meteorites fall to earth. He's searching for the missing piece of the jigsaw in what a stranger might or might not say.

That's what loneliness can do to people, kick away the usual props of the day. Finch doesn't try to hide it. I'm back inside the cottage before he gets a chance to contextualise his thoughts into words, before he can contaminate me with his need.

I'd an idea something like this might happen the week before I left London so abruptly. I'd spent most of the day with Peter Branwitz, at a meeting and then studying the final draughts for the designs in one of those chain coffee shops that dot London. By six I'd had enough. Branwitz could see that. I didn't have to spell it out that my mind had closed down to all concepts of work. We parted at Leicester Square, Branwitz spontaneously jumping into a peddle-rickshaw for the journey to Charing Cross where he caught his train home. Off he went laughing and waving through the early-evening crowds, shouting back that it was fun.

I could have done the same, taken a rickshaw to Tottenham Court Road and then a Central line train home. That's what I'd yearned for all afternoon, an undelayed train home to Corinne and the cats. But oddly I turned towards Leicester Square station, not knowing why. Hawkers from the Chinese massage shops touched my arm as I passed and invited me inside. I walked on barely conscious of what they were saying. They must have thought I'd been drinking. I didn't know where I was going or why I was entering a

Piccadilly line station when I should have been making for the Central line.

I only travelled a few stops, irked by the crowds, emerging at Kings Cross. I travelled upwards on an escalator, just another faceless evening commuter, taking a final series of tired steps to the street. I hadn't been there for years, had no reason go there. Occasionally a journey necessitated a change of lines at Kings Cross, another walk along another underground interchange tunnel indistinguishable from all the other underground tunnels. Somewhere in the back of my mind I must have made a note to exit one day just to see the new extension to Saint Pancras station, but I'd never got around to it. That evening after leaving Peter Branwitz I got around to it, when I really ought to have been going home to Greenford.

I walked among tourists from St. Pancras to King Cross station, as far as the beginning of Pentonville Road. The poetry of Kings Cross is now more likely to be spoken in French or Japanese. Before it was street-junkies screaming at each other down York Road.

Do you think you can help me? Someone asked me that just outside the station. I barely glanced at him as I walked on. I assumed the man was just another beggar haunting London's rail stations. Afterwards I realised he hadn't actually begged me. Maybe he was just looking for directions, or local information. For a minute I thought about returning to find him, to ask him what he wanted. But he'd have been swallowed up by the flow of people.

What are you thinking about? Do others love you enough? What makes you lonely? Do you wonder if others will remember you when you're gone? Do you miss those friends who are not around? When last did someone say they love you? Some questions you'll not be asked in somewhere like Kings Cross. I paused among the crowds to notice the sounds of the station, remembering it was one of the first parts of London I got to know. Cars passing, someone laughing. Luggage pulled on wheels along the pavements. More cars passing. The impersonality of large cities changes people. If you mention that to friends they'd say there's nothing anyone can do about it. And they'd look at you, angry that you brought it up in the first place.

Instead of catching a train home to Corinne and the cats I hung around the mall in St Pancras, thinking how they linked the area to the soul of France by eurutunnel trains. The link to France will end too one day. Everything is change. The only constant is human perception ... and human suffering.

For moments in the flux and expectation of a rail station the future seemed possible. But within a second it seemed impossible again. I texted Corinne, said the meeting was extended, that I was running late.

In the Kings Cross in 1987 I was just another commuter making my way home on a train. It could have happened to me. I must have taken that old wooden escalator on the evening it happened. I read the inquest papers at the time in Camden library, about how three doctors at the scene testified that they'd found a human torso, a foot and part of a skull at the scene. But none of the body parts belonged to the thirty one bodies recorded as having died. To this day the body parts are unclaimed, the identity of the thirty second victim a mystery. Perhaps someone is still waiting for him to come home.

At a burger-kiosk I overheard a fragment of conversation about the Marquis de Sade between a fast-food migrant worker without much English and a guy who introduced himself as a psychiatric patient on a day-pass. In the context of that moment it made sense. Corinne texted me just about then, worried about the evening's dinner arrangements. She'd been trying out new recipes.

I didn't know what I was doing there, idling with time, trying to think clearly through a wedge of mental pain. Nobody belongs there but yet everyone belongs there. Nothing happens there but eventually everything happens there. People passing looked content because they were living in the philosophy of movement. No time to record success or failure. Only constant movement mattered.

I tried to work out what was happening to me but couldn't. If two strangers who'd lost their memories met there it'd be the perfect place to meet. The past has no meaning in busy London rail-stations. As I climbed stiffly from a mall-bench and began the journey home to Corinne I didn't know what was wrong with me. I knew it had something to do with the face from the past I'd seen on the underground a day or two before. I had no idea about the implications of what I'd seen. But I guessed I'd soon find out.

Chapter 3

How repulsive Marco looked behind the desk of the Hotel Eugene Plasky, a carafe of Chateau de la Tuilerie at one elbow, the empty bottle tipped on its side on the floor. The words that passed between us on that first meeting were indifferent and brief. He dug a solitary key from the pocket of his pin-striped waistcoat and tossed it on the reception desk and then jerked a thumb in the direction of a doorway leading off the reception area.

Room two ... the end of the corridor.

It's hard to describe Marco; or just about possible to describe him. The word grotesque wouldn't be unfair. He was grotesque in an obscene way. He looked like he was sneering at the world and everyone in it, yet he never actually sneered. His teeth were filthy and gold-capped in places, lips deeply chapped. His lips were chapped enough to bleed but they never bled, at least not that I noticed. He spoke American-English as if he'd spent time in America. Yet he said he'd never visited that country. His eyes were often vacant and voice slurred as if he used drugs but at the same time he was sharp, as if he could see around corners. Some said he was Moldavian or Bulgarian or a Bosnian Roma. Others said he was born in Malta and brought up in a German circus. But he himself said he came from Brussels and that he'd always come from Brussels. That's all I can say about Marco. If I think about him for a second longer I swear I'll vomit up the lining of my stomach ...

I dragged the suitcase through a dark corridor that stank of a heaving drain. The room was little more than a dusty arrangement of broken furniture. The ceiling was full of tiny cracks as if a madman had stuck the amputated legs of a thousand spiders into chaotic patterns. Dead flies shriveled on an empty shelf. I pulled the suitcase through mouse droppings, poking the single bed with the toe of one shoe. That moment is isolated, lifted like a finger-print from a crime-scene. Not that it's a revelation, not that I haven't known for years. It's simple, if I hadn't have met Marco I wouldn't have done what I did.

When the facts change, people change too. A famous economist or politician once said that. Can't remember which one, or the context in which he said it. People change their tune constantly, when the circumstances are more favourable to do so. In the servitude of a national cause people act how they wouldn't normally act. A dictator is exonerated, a sadistic torture-murderer from a tropical junta is forgiven. Only his victims and the families of his victims are angry, but they are not important enough to have a choice in the matter.

In defence of a cause people are forgiven. Prisoners are released early, pardoned in acknowledgment that the crimes were for a cause. I pondered it night after night, the forgiveness required. The circumstances had changed so radically, from the degraded thought-life of an unformed man to the sated normality of suburban

London. That degree of change must excuse an element of the crimes in question. I'd changed wholly. If one of the very few people who knew me in Brussels during that year had met me later in London they wouldn't have recognised me. They couldn't have reasoned that the unformed man from the Hotel Eugene Plasky was the same man living in the western suburbs of London with a wife and a trimmed garden hedge. They'd see that the second man couldn't be rationally held to account for the actions of the first man.

The only thing missing was a cause. I'd no cause then, as I've no cause now. There was no cause to cause injury or kill for. There were only the diminished actions of the unformed man. The only possible causes were an obsession for beauty. Men who'd have seen Sonia would understand. She had an effect on men. Nobody who knew her could be surprised to hear that she died like she did, so young, at the hands of a man who loved her.

Before Sonia there was only Ginni. On the first night here by the sea I visualised them both in a perfect frame of memory. I met Ginni as she hurried through the ground-floor entrance from the street. She paused, as if by an a priori prompt she knew she had to speak with me. How people stared at her – fishy Cyclops eye at the keyhole. To see Ginni's beauty meant seeing beyond the surgical stitching on her face and neck. We joked about the hotel, about how we found ourselves in such a dive. She reached out to touch my arm, ignoring how I stared at her scars.

I turn from the view out the cottage back-window because nothing can supersede its beauty. I'm searching the past for yet more truth, for a reason as to why I stayed at the Hotel Eugene Plasky for longer than the necessary night or two. Stretching on the divan with only the ceiling as a distraction it's coming back. The coast is working more of its magic, soothing away decades as if such an impasse of time is insignificant.

She wore mittens in summer, said home spanned a panoply of cities and countries. In the few days that followed on we bumped into each other in the corridors and just outside the hotel front-door. She didn't make an excuse to hurry away like the girls I met usually did, reaching out from somewhere beyond that maimed face. She helped me to pronounce French words and street-names, told me about the cheap places she'd found to eat and shop. She wanted to know about jewellery, about the processes of a studio.

I must have spoken about the Korchnoi-Karpov match, about how I'd been following the chess coverage in the London Telegraph as they sold it at three times its London price at a kiosk just off the Grand Place. I'd never been alone with a girl in her room before that scarred saviour unlocked the double-locks to my heart. She'd asked me to drop off one of the London papers to her in the evening.

The room was marked by the hotel's universal neglect, a dry-rot ceiling and unfilled holes in the walls where electric sockets used to be. We laughed about the noises from the water-pipes, comparing the respective rattles in our rooms. I worried if her skin might chaff or cause her to cry out in pain if it came into contact with someone else's skin. She ignored the newspaper I brought, gesturing for me to sit by her on the bed. Apart from a suitcase on the top of a wardrobe there was no evidence of her occupation of the room. She looked around her and laughed. What a hoot staying in such a dump, she said. I can't wait to tell my friends about it.

I didn't hear the other things she said, about university in England and an academic year she needed to complete; or only heard them abstractly. I was lost in the lightness of her voice, in the beauty beyond the scars. When she touched my hand the tension was a living force within the hotel walls.

She sat there like the youngest sister of a universal clan of burns' victims, an extended family of pain. Her mouth found my mouth. When I undressed and stood in front of her she said nothing, just took me between her lips. We stumbled between the bed-covers, poking each other with elbows and knees until we found the needed position. She undressed beneath the covers, hiding the totality of her marks and scars. She asked me to draw the blinds on the windows, the evening darkening.

She guided my pathetic gropings as we celebrated her perfection with the love-rite, my hands nervous in the dark, unsure of where to touch. Her buttocks were deeply pitted, sites for the skin-crafts. I came for the first time inside a woman and slumped beside her on the narrow bed, all the accumulated tension of the years blown away in seconds.

Your face and neck, I said as tenderly as I could. Was it an accident?

She laughed softly as yellow light from street-lamps dissected the room from a gap in the window-blinds.

It's okay, she said. I don't talk about it.

If we followed the light from the window, we'd find heaven.

Don't be silly, she said closing her eyes. This is heaven.

My eyes are closed too, in the lighthouse cottage, holding onto an image of Ginni distorted by time. But then quickly it's gone, leaving the usual ache and loss. What we had is gifted once or twice in life. Typically it passes before we realize we have it in our grasp. I turn again to the window in the back-room of the cottage, to face the inquisition of the sea.

Chapter 4

In the grey light of the basement of the Goudron Studio M.Goudron told me about the chess café on Rue des Chartreux when I mentioned the Korchnoi-Karpov match. He volunteered to guide me to the Scharbeek on a Sunday to visit Magritte's old house on Rue des Mimoses. I looked at stupidly, not knowing what to say.

He sniffed the remnant of the previous night's alcohol on my breath in the first weeks and looked into my bloodshot eyes. Then he lost interest and asked nothing about my life outside the basement studio. The work began with the prison at Saint Gilles a backdrop in the cityscape. In the morning M.Goudron wore an artisan's apron with plastic safety goggles pushed back on his graying helmet of hair. He'd ask his handful of workers if we'd like an espresso before we began. Then for the remainder of the day he'd work us like dogs.

In the first week he'd handed me a slip of paper with an address where the studio's apprentices stayed. The accommodation was cheap but supervised strictly by a matron with set times for lights-out. I took the address and nodded and thanked M.Goudron. The address was close to a street by the North station famous for whore-houses. Everyone knew how to find that street but I didn't bother looking. That's the glaring sin, the step omission that led to the crime that's brought me here all these years later.

That evening after making love with Ginni I called around to her room and knocked on her door. The door opened and a man stood there with red lines on his arms as if he'd been scratching at a skin condition. Barefoot and bare-chested, one finger probing the edges of a growth the size of a golf-ball on his cheek.

Where's Ginni?

Do I know you?

I said where's Ginni? The girl who lives here.

He looks at me blankly then banged the door shut in my face, clicking the lock shut with emphasis. The rasp of metal slotting home terminated the conversation. I ran back along the corridor and down the stairs towards the reception. At the reception desk Marco shrugged his shoulders and said she'd checked out that morning and didn't leave a forwarding address. He perked up visibly at the sight of a guest distressed in reception.

She couldn't have, I said.

I know nothing about her ... except that she's gone.

She must have left contact details when she checked in.

She didn't ... I didn't ask her any questions.

He gestured cryptically with his hands and grinned. He'd have stood there for hours if he could, lapping up the misery, breathing it in. Even as puerile as I was then I could see he was enjoying it, see how he thrived on suffering. I walked back to my room in a daze, trying to take it in. Ginni was gone, our last words spoken in the surreal, the moments too precious to be tainted by logic. Then she was gone. Ginni's laugh, Marco's words, are frozen in the present, the fragments revealed in a single blur of memory. The sea is a merciful confessor, sedating the mind and illuminating the conclusions.

The wicker-chair by the back window of the lighthouse cottage turns time inside out. There's no other reason for coming here. It's how it is meant to be. The last days and nights in London are clarified, the yellow safety line on Central line platforms. It didn't end then because of the existence of the sea. The sea was always one final hope.

On the last evening in London the train rattled to a point in the journey where westbound trains slow, the beginnings of the suburbs. Wheels switched and grinded in the points' lever, catching metal yelping, the train shuddering to a halt at Ealing Broadway. The concept of the sea lapped on thoughts of self-destruction like a saviour.

The sea and the lighthouse pick the scabs to reveal why I stayed longer than a night or two at the Hotel Eugene Plasky. After Ginni had gone there was no reason to stay there. But by then I'd spotted the young Gypsy Sonia rushing in and out of the building. She wasn't any older than seventeen or eighteen, eyes daring the world.

Shaken by memories of the first sightings of Sonia I grab my duffel-bag and place my phone in the deepest pocket and make for the sea, craving the distances extending beyond the headlands. Outside the day is fresher than the clear blue of sky suggests. I walk and breath in deeply and pretend not to notice Pat Finch waving in my direction as if we're bonded by blood. His presence is startling, an unwanted input of kindness. It's too late to cover my head with the hood of the duffel for to block out the peripheries. I can only wonder what I have to do to steer clear of him.

He's wilder in spirit than earlier on, sandy hair uncombed like a difficult schoolboy, giddier than his children. His two pre-puberty girls have jumped into the back-seats of the family hatchback and are impatient for the sea. Their father calls out their destination to me, a nearby swimming cove with a sandy beach. Neither of the girls resemble him and there's no obvious likeness between them and their mother either.

Pat Finch's wife Jemma is hurrying from the back-door of the bungalow to the opened boot of her car, carrying towels and a pink set of water-wings. She looks too harassed by time to form an opinion on the abstract. I've met her a thousand times in London, or women very like her. She's too busy to say anything but the briefest hello. She's frowning as if she's argued against swimming on such a fresh day but lost out to numbers. There's a very subtle bitterness in her grey eyes. Pat Finch tries to please her with evidence of my normality, my suitability as a neighbor. He's waiting for his wife to join him, he blurts out.

We've only just met but yet there's a conspiratorial dimension to our relationship, as if he's protecting me against misunderstandings. A mother of young girls needs to hear an incidental word or two of re-assurance in these times; strange men never viewed as so potentially strange. Jemma Finch is busy with the preparations, arbitrating a gripe between her girls. She smiles at me tightly as she packs in the towels.

She looks older than her husband, although they're probably the one age. She hasn't bothered with the details of the feminine, no mascara or foundation. She's as nature made her; manly in anorak and jeans, shoulders drooping like a tired wrestler. How easy the unkinder assumptions appear, the lazier conceptions of her humanity. Without the common sense of Corinne and the nebulous social norms of London to hide behind I'm vulnerable around Jemma Finch. I sense she dislikes me, that she can sense I'm wondering what it'd be like to sleep beside her listening to the gusts of breath and watching the powerful chest and shoulders rising and falling with the rhythms of sleep. Come along with us, her husband is saying. If you don't feel like swimming it's a nice place to sit.

I demure with a facial gesture and a quick movement of one hand; imagining what his wife is thinking about a stranger tagging along, impassively eyeing her and her girls squeezing into swimsuits, trying not to let the towels drop. I'm heading for the village, I say. Might stop off for a drink.

They can understand that, the needs of the belly and the panacea of the Irish pub. If I mention food and drink often enough they might even get to like me. He wants to drop me off in the village though the swimming cove is in an opposite direction. The sea-air, I say breathing in with exaggeration and walking on.

Before I go he insists I say hello to his girls, Aoife and Ellie. He can't grasp that I haven't come here to act out weary social niceties. I make it brief, say the quickest hello possible through an opened window of the car.

The children come across as normal in their social development, neither precocious nor withdrawn. Finch is very proud of them, mentioning an equestrian medal the older girl won weeks earlier. Neither of them are pretty, both with the same lifeless sandy hair of their father. One of them has a turned-up nose so distinct that it borders on disfigurement. Her front teeth are prominent too – troubles ahead for those first teenage dances, tears on the pillow.

As I make for the coastal walk to the village Finch wants to know if I'd like to call around that evening to look through his telescope. I look at him in amazement. I've had more contact with him in just one day than with our neighbours in Greenford for the past decade. I point in the direction of the village and Finch understands the gesture; a man's necessity to move on about the chores of the day.

In the distance a marsh-hawk or buzzard is flying in the direction of the sloblands. Earlier what looked like a peregrine or sea-eagle circled the lighthouse and a black redstart contemplated in the mud of the strand. I learnt about birds in the wetlands of Barnes and regret not remembering to bring binoculars. In the first minutes under the spell of the lighthouse I'm sure I seen a purple sandpiper on the headland.

The village is devoid of art or abstraction, with nothing on sale only what's necessary. Hollywood dvds and cut-price airports and lifestyle magazines line the shelves of a mini-superstore. I walk up the one-street village and then back again. It's a village of functionality, without distractions to subvert me from the reason I am here.

In the largest of the village pubs there's a hot-plate and dining area in an annex. The girl serving wears a silver stud in her lower lip and doesn't bother with eye-contact as I order. She seems suspicious that I'm on my own, at a pained distance from the world. It's hard not to imagine her spitting on my chicken-wings when nobody's looking. Out through a long window I see the car-park busy with vehicles from the Rosslare ferry, campervans and caravans on tow. Nobody asks where I'm from or where I'm heading for. Nobody asks me anything except questions to do with my dinner.

An older bar-worker is motherly towards the girl with the stud in her lip. She also regards me unsympathetically, scenting out a stranger with no status in the world she inhabits. Both women are generous towards the locals, quick to talk intimately about village life. It's not friendliness but the rules of survival. To swim in a small pond one must negotiate the same conversational engagement with the same trivial retreads of conversation. And then do it again, and again. They look at me without pity, look at me as an outsider as much as any outsider who'd never before set foot in Ireland.

At the nearest table a family from the English North country are absorbed in the strop of their youngest child. Corinne would have spoken just like them before university and years in London moderated her voice to middle English.

I push the plate of food away from me, too angry to eat. I'm angry about why I'm here, about what happened in

Brussels. The chicken is rubbery anyhow, the texture of the mashed potato that of a sponge. I'm keen to go, to escape the glances of the two women serving, the stigma of a solitary table.

The older worker reads my departure and is quick to the till. For a moment I consider asking her if there is a problem. Was it something I done or did she seriously think I'd leave without paying? If the crucible of remembrance in the lighthouse cottage wasn't waiting for me I might say something to regret. I take control as she takes the money. She's dismissive as she hands back the change, already looking towards a diner musing at the hot-plate.

Outside I hate myself more than I'd ever hated myself, even more than on that evening on the Central line when I inched within an inch or two of the train. Having shared so much with Corinne separation from her is a torture by time. In the village people regard me as if my solitude is an established fact, as if my existence without Corinne has meaning.

Among the village buildings all sight of the sea has vanished. Further on there's a dull grey stain through a hedgerow marking its presence. Outside another village pub a woman with blue tints in her hair and wearing a high-vis bib is rattling a charity bucket. There's no decent way of getting past her without giving so I dig out loose change. She's uncertain as I approach, unsure if she should seek out my charity. We're collecting for cancer, she says as I drop the coins into the bucket and slip past.

Inside it's busy with room at the counter for one or two. A lad of nineteen or twenty is at the pumps and he serves me promptly. They are showing the provincial hurling final on the television; strong hurling talk at the bar. The two men on one side are discussing an incident before the weekend before.

They had to call the Guards out.

Drugs probably.

He must 'a been on somethin'. Runnin' up an' down the village at hour at that hour.

Waving a knife you say.

That's not normal.

No. Not yet it isn't.

They ignore me. One or two nod indifferently. The young barman is not yet ruined by life, telling me about the match. I take whisky with water. A man from further along the counter is singing a verse about Vandeleur's militia storming to the defense of Ross. As abruptly as he begins to sing, he's silent again. I listen in to the fragments of conversations and it's obvious nothing happens here other than church draws, whist-drives and anniversary masses and the occasional madman running loose with a knife.

A rung with a red woolen hat pulled over his ears studies me from a nearby table, one eye closing to maximize concentration. The top part of his body is swaying slightly as he minds a dead pint. Hey boss, he says. Did you see the match?

No … any good?

You missed the match .. you couldn't be a Wexfordman!

He gropes for his pint glass, misses it, growls and then tries again. The inadequacy of the space he takes up in the world is remarkable. His jacket looks more plastic than leather, a hole the size of a fist in one sleeve. He grips his pint and tries to stand. The young barman is monitoring the runt from behind the taps, taking on the age-old role of responsibility over the inebriate. He begins to whine about the match and I turn in towards the counter, catching the sympathetic eye of the boy serving. Noel, the boy calls out. You've been warned often enough about bothering customers.

Others turn from the counter to burden the runt with frowns. There's a tiredness to the process as if they've all been through it one too many times before. The young barman mentions a final warning. There's nothing in the public house that brings me closer to the reason I'm here. The men ignore the run and exchange even stronger hurling talk, clubbing each other with words. I nod to the boy behind the counter and leave almost as unnoticed as when I entered.

Outside there's nothing only the sea and the lighthouse cottage with which to piece together the necessary fragments of memory. What has any man but his own ability to fathom out his problems? I walk on, to an inquisition of recall at the very edge of land, to the hope of getting home to Corinne as a man purged of conscience.

Chapter 5

A drunk screamed in my face in a bar in Ixcelles, veins bulging on his temple and forehead like burrowing tape-worms. An unknown part of Brussels. a barman in an apron waving a billy-club in the air. Outside it was just another drunken street, buildings spinning, a metro-train to catch to Porte de Hal or Porte Namur. The squalid room in the Hotel Eugene Plasky waited at the end of the night. And the hope that somehow Ginni might show up again, or that I'd see Sonia hurrying through the ground-floor corridors. I isolate the moment caught up in a spell cast by the sea, feel the weight of that unformed man alone in a foreign city.

The sequence of mental images dredged from the events in Brussels all those years ago in are dispersed by the cry of seagulls. The gulls' screams are unnatural, as if they've been infected with aviary madness from a polluted pool. The pressure of memory feels closer to mental dysfunction than any other pressure. It takes the view of the sea through the lighthouse-cottage window to re-contextualize the morning. The intrusion of what happened back then dominates the cottage interior like an unspeakable infestation. And then people say we're free moral agents in a world of continual choices. What they really mean is that they're pleased with the measure of fate handed down to them.

The night before a sea-mist transformed the peninsula into a universe of porous uncertainty. I rang Corinne to hear tiredness weighting on her voice. She spoke flatly about the school-inspection, about how unreasonable the inspectors were. Unenthusiastically she broke down the events of the day. My eyes were closing as she described the routines of Greenford, the sea a narcotic. I only wished to describe the other-worldliness of the coast. It's hard to say what annoyed her most, the obstinate school-inspectors, or my distantness.

The pieces on the chessboard in the backroom of the cottage are stalled in an impasse from the Korchnoi-Karpov match. The games in Baguio City dragged on so long that the world championships scheduled for October of that year were jeopardised. The first seven games were drawn but Karpov won game eight after Korchnoi spent forty five minutes on one move. They spoke of adjourning the games to a closed room after Korchnoi claimed the para-psychologist Zukhar tried to hypnotise him. Korchnoi described Karpov's eleventh move in the tenth game as a move played only once in a century. After ten games and nine draws Karpov went ahead by a solitary game.

Shaking off a flu-like effect of thinking excessively about the past I make for the outdoors, to the seduction of the sea. The coast is slipping free of the influence of a heavy grey blanket of morning. There's a cinematic moment at the door of the cottage, as if I'm stepping into a one-man film-set involving panoramics of the sea. The sloop with the vivid red and white beams has vanished, the props used to secure it in dry-dock stacked neatly against the sea-wall. The walking possibilities are boundless. If a walker is brave enough for the rocky outgrops separating each strand it's possible to walk to the provincial boundary.

By the sea the terror of London's underground train platforms fades to practically nothing. Only a few months back three people jumped in one day at various stations throughout the metropolis. It wasn't reported in the media as someone must have decided it was bad for morale. I only knew about it because I'd spent a long day travelling on the tube and heard the three separate announcements. Delays due to a passenger under a train; that's how they phrased it. They sounded smug, pleased they had a plausible reason for the delays. Three in one day. Others the same week no doubt. And on the slow hills of North London the ominous sight of 'suicide bridge'. It's a feat to have made it as far as the sea.

Again Pat Finch surprises me on the headland, as I'm staring at the sea. Loneliness precedes him, the neediness that he's apparently unashamed of. He's hesitant in his interruption, like as if he's disturbed me as I'm waiting for Neptune to rise from the waves with the defining revelation. He jogs the final distance between us.

The conditions for the telescope were brilliant last night. You missed it!

We're almost used to each other already, lapsing into our respective roles.

Another time.

It's an eighty mill refractor with no dead-spots. If you don't set the mount right it blocks the view at certain angles.

He's bouncing on his heels as he speaks, proud of his telescope, desperate to get a chance to show it off.

You'll love it here, he says. It's everything a man needs. And to think I nearly walked away from it once. Did all the paperwork for Canada but didn't get enough emigration points.

I shrug, unsure of what he wants from me. His energy is boyish. One can imagine him volunteering for a NASA voyage to Mars. Grimacing as the radiation mutates his cell-structures, his bones excreting calcium after days of near-weightlessness, his cardio-vascular system in meltdown from the want of gravity. Through blinding headaches he'd report his progress to ground-control – the first Irishman in space.

Just as well I didn't get enough points," he says laughing. As I met the wife shortly afterwards ... It was meant to be.

He turns to examine my profile and smiling briefly I nod again. Then he points to the sea, to where he says the coastguard found a floating body earlier in the year. I try to imagine death in that guise, the vulnerability of the human form in the sea-temperatures. On a clear night the unfortunate individual would have had a wondrous view of the stars before he closed his eyes forever.

It's a pity your wife can't be here, he says shyly. I'd say she'd like the views.

She'd love the views.

Next week you say she's coming?

He thinks I'm in the dog-house, cast out from the woman I love, playing out my role in a domestic drama. The situation he imagines I'm in has him thinking at more than one level, as if working through the most recent conversation he's has with his wife. Geese are making for the sloblands in co-ordinated flights. I look from the geese to the section of the sea where Finch is pointing.

See that launch out there? I know the people onboard.

It's impossible to see that far with the naked eye. The shoreland is incomplete without binoculars. He's exaggerating his knowledge of the sea in a one-man performance before an audience of one. I barely know him but already he knows I design jewellery for a living and am married to a woman named Corinne. He knows more about me than my neighbours in Greenford know. It must be the power of the sea, working like a truth-serum. Unlike London there's nowhere to hide here, nowhere to perfect an act of indifference. It has to be down to isolation and boredom, this interest Pat Finch is taking in my existence. His questions lack malice and sophistication, almost child-like in their orientation.

Jemma's favourite bracelet has a broken clasp, he says after an interlude of silence.

I'd like to help Pat ... but I've no tools, no workbench.

He weights up my response shrewdly as we both look out to sea. He never mentions the broken bracelet again. How graciously he accepts his allocation of fate, the manly wife and the little girls, one with a disfigured nose. He'd die for them without a second's hesitation.

I can drop you off where you need to go, he says cheerfully.

That's okay ... I wouldn't miss these walks for the world.

If the skies are clear tonight you should call over. You won't be disappointed by this telescope.

Sure ... why not?

He looks happy with that answer and hurries away with more purpose. His minutes and hours are compressed with meaning, but yet he's unfathomably lonely, empty of a key element. There's no other reason why he's seeking me out so fervently.

Out to sea the weather's changing, malevolent winds whipping up the sea-surface. It's incomprehensible that people are waiting on Central line platforms for crowded trains, putting up with shoves from all directions. If they really knew about the sea they'd abandon their struggle to cover meagre spans of subterranean distance. If they really knew the sea they'd abandon towns and cities forever too. Only after a couple of days I'm beginning to understand the language that the sea seduces the animate with, the codes whispered to the dreams of those slumbering in its presence.

There's a succinct text-message from Corinne. Succinct and dispassionate, lacking in the warmth that defines our love. By the gaps in the conversation when we speak on the phone I can hear she's not taking my absence magnanimously. It's pointless worrying her unnecessarily by mentioning that the absence of train-platforms are a major factor in my personal survival.

At the beginning of the peninsula, on a path of rocks leading to the lighthouse, the commissioners of Irish lights have hammered up a warning sign. The surface of the peninsula is dangerously rocky. From the prominent rocks the Ross light is visible and one can even see as far as Tuskar in good conditions. If I make it out of here alive I'll design and craft a special ring for Corinne, a celebration of our love. For our twentieth anniversary I used seventeen point seven grams of eighteen carat gold and two point fifteen grams of diamond to make a ring she loves so much that she wears it proudly on the important occasions.

On that last day in London Peter Branwitz called me three times on my private number; more than he'd usually call in a month. We'd been working closely on jewellery designs, spending more time together than ever before. We travelled on the Central line mid-morning, shoulders pressed together in side-by-side seats. They designed these seats when the average Londoner was the size of a midget, he said.

The day before I'd edged an inch or two beyond the yellow safety line on a tube platform as a train arrived, leaning forward into the blasts of displaced air. The train barely missed me. I expected the driver or station staff to make a scene. But nobody said a word, or barely seemed to notice. I glanced at Branwitz, tried to reach out from what was happening inside me.

I see someone jumped this morning.

Another one. Apparently London has more jumpers than New York or Paris.

Branwitz yawned disinterestedly as the train rails squealed, switches on the line meeting the rotational inertia of the sleepers, changing the direction of the train's termination. Grids and rods grinding on truncated surfaces, the trains always on hand to mangle flesh and bone. It wasn't that Peter Branwitz didn't care, or was indifferent towards the ordinary feelings of others. It was just London, in the midst of another working day. It wasn't the time to expand on the vulnerability of one's humanity.

He didn't say much, but the second or two he added to the pause between his words said everything. As we parted at Bond Street he said he knew a leading Harley Street specialist.

What kind of specialist?

Headaches. You've been talking about headaches that keep you awake at night. What kind of specialist did you think I meant?

I nodded, past caring, past the point of trying to follow what he meant. It wasn't until I made it past the check-in at Heathrow that the headaches dissipated. And my pulse normalised. Corinne begged me to go to casualty but medicine wasn't the answer. I needed to get out of London.

Friends texted and rang, prompted by Corinne. They assumed it all pertained to work, the pressuring of Peter Branwitz. I said London wasn't the place to be, that I'd things on my mind. It happened too abruptly for to have time to analyse the events that led to the airport. I'd lost whatever relationships I'd had with Ireland through decades of absence, so it came as a surprise it was the first place I thought of escaping to.

Before the plane touched down at Dublin it was apparent that I hadn't got away with what I always thought I'd gotten away with. It brushed the years aside as if they'd not happened. It was growing like the rudest cancer within my thought processes. I contemplated the very little I knew about court-room and legal procedure, the phenomena of modern incarceration, cell-doors banging thunderously. And the more I thought about it, the more it looked like the only hope lay in the direction of the mothering sea.

Chapter 6

Out there in the world women, many of them beautiful, adorn themselves with jewellery from these hands. The same hands that caused all that pain, hands that have brought on this separation from everything of meaning in life. I stare at them as if they belong to someone else, a stranger oʀ a deranged escapee on the run. Pouring the first coffee of the morning I search my mind for the defining moment when I lost control. The actual names are impossible to pin down with memory, that cipher of streets south of the Petit ring in Brussels.

Through a block of mental pain I picture the foyer of the Hotel Eugene Plasky, brown walls and dirt congealing in the joins between the white floor-tiles. I see Sonia at the reception-desk, whispering intimate words to Marco or hurrying to the rooms on the top floor. Her flowing black skirts and dresses to the ankle, with a split up one side showing the bare sallow skin. Once she wore a white rose in her hair, a black lace scarf billowing from her shoulders. With low tops she showed the orbs of her breasts, an edge of nipple exposed. She looked at me like the whores of Rue d'Aerschot looked at me, measuring the depths of lust.
That's where I sometimes tried to find her, in the red-lit windows of Rue d'Aerschot, expecting to see her in the tightest leotard, fishing men in with the movement of an index finger. But I never found her there, nor in the streets or corners where the unlicensed whores worked either. The Hotel Eugene Plasky was the only hope in the world of seeing Sonia. Once I tried to speak to her as she entered the doorway of the hotel. Her sweat mingled with the smell of cheap perfume. She smiled, showing a chipped front tooth. I needed to say so much

but nothing came out beyond a kind of grunt. We were standing so close together I caught a full garlic aroma from between her lips. Then she laughed before hurrying on, the laugh travelling from a long way down her throat.

Once I followed her into the street, into what was once the old Marolles' district of the city. At the entrance to Porte de Hal station she paused to draw a black scarf tighter around her shoulders. Men turned to notice her as they passed. If she'd have looked over one shoulder she'd have seen me following her, noticed how surreptitiously I moved. She'd have sensed it; women always do. She's have known there was something wrong.

The room-charges at the Hotel Eugene Plasky were so cheap it was as easy to stay as to find somewhere else. In the hallway a bore from Bremen on a downbeat road-trip tried to sell me grass. A Bruxsellois kicked out by his wife swearing late into the night in the room next to mine. The expected distractions. They didn't mean anything in themselves. By then, only seeing Sonia as she hurried in and out of the hotel entailed anything remotely connected to meaningfulness.

A mental picture of the Hotel Eugene Plasky is transposed vividly in the back-window of the lighthouse-cottage, saturated in a malaise of spirit. Once a young traveller with a rucksack complained of the smell in the hotel rooms, the heaving drain from the back-yard. Marco shrugged from behind the hotel's reception desk, turned down his lower lip, doodling indolently on the back of an envelope. It's Belgium, he said quietly. It's not easy trying to run a business under so many layers of government.

That's how Marco spoke to people, quietly, without any fuss, pointing out the abstract reasons as to why the hotel was in such a dire condition. Nobody, man or woman, ever wished to argue with him, or speak with him longer than absolutely necessary. Usually they thanked him, moved on, avoided him from then on.

As the mood of morning alters with a turbulence of grey shifting skies I lift the 'Encyclopedia of Chess Openings' from the table propped against the back-window of the cottage. On the twenty fifth game of the Korchnoi-Karpov match the score stood at four-two in favour of Karpov. Korchnoi had conjured up a draw from nothing. A chess correspondent in Baguio City compared Korchnoi's escape to a drunk jumping from a plane, unsure if he'd a rucksack or parachute on his back. By the twenty eight game Karpov needed only one further win for the world title. The chess correspondent reported that they'd already noted defeat in Korchnoi's expressions, signs he'd already accepted that defeat was only a matter of time.

The greyness of the morning is an unavoidable portent of the weather to come. There's a gale warning on the radio, a mention of wind speeds of up to fifty off the peninsula. The mist restricts the view to somewhere around a nautical mile, certainly not much more than that. It's a morning for heavy swells, the sea breaching the headland in a breathless performance. Through the mist guillemots or possibly razorbills are flying gloriously towards the Saltee Islands.

The morning is dominated by the sea-mists and the absence of a text-message from Corinne. To be without her is unbearable. I'm greedy for her, hoping she'll text or call. More than that I hate this deluge of guilt, the impulses that have brought me here.

Corinne doesn't believe I'm capable of doing anything to actually cause this guilt, assumes it's all to do with an unconscious craving for suffering. I don't actually say anything to the contrary, allow the assumption to sit, the Freudian view that civilisation by its definition constructs an unconscious force of guilt. In Corinne's eyes the problem is civilisation, not what I may have done or left undone. She mentioned a friend of a friend, a post-Kleinian analyst I'd met once or twice socially. His designer spectacles looked ridiculous on a man so fundamentally uncool. He remained apart from others for remarkably long spans of time at the parties Corinne sometimes coerced me to attend. An unusually awkward man who paused uncertainly in the middle of his sentences, as if floundering in a confusing inner-world. I wondered what Corinne hoped he might do for me.

The sea-mists are transforming the coast-side into an ethereal world, views from the headland fading. On the very first day on the coast, out beyond the reefs of seaweed, a flare fizzled skywards from Raven Point. It was if the sea was waiting patiently for me to arrive and had acknowledged my arrival.

The village is lifeless, shrouded in mist. People climbing from cars in front of the village shops somehow bring to mind blinkered and mute pawns pushed around by unseen forces. A few of them acknowledge me with brief, impersonal nods. They're barely curious about my appearance amongst them. They look through me after an initial glance to confirm I'm nobody of importance. The pub where I ate the previous day is advertising a vegetarian breakfast with a sign in one of its windows. As I step inside to investigate both women from yesterday's dinner are talking loudly to each other. They're visibly disappointed to see me again, as if I've presented them with a significant problem by showing up on two consecutive days.

A man in green wellington boots and a trilby blackened by dirt is the only other customer present. He's talking softly to himself, looking from the ceiling to a faraway point beyond the cafeteria's windows. He scratches at two or three days of silver-white growth on his chin, a misalignment of his nose giving him the look of a tramp. He's somehow familiar even though I've never seen him before, as if he too has been cast out by the new Ireland.

The grease from the cooking pan drift in a revolting taint of scent throughout the interior, so instead of anything cooked I order a cold sandwich and a coffee. Ordering I notice a scab forming by the face-stud worn by the younger bar-worker. Then I remember the times we're in and look away quickly. People misunderstand looks from men; even a man as ineffective in appearance as I clearly must be.

The countryman scrapes his chair unnecessarily on the floor as he rises, lifting his trilby in a comical gesture of goodbye. In a blur of mountain dialect he bids all present the very best of what the day has to offer. He'd be the ideal man to while away whisky hours in the snug of a crossroads pub, at an unusual day in the Ireland of my boyhood like Good Friday or Stephens Day, when men naturally turned to drink. As he leaves and carefully closes the door after him the younger bar-worker mimics a phrase he used and then sniggers behind one hand. Both women are laughing from their stomachs, feeding off each other's grins.

They're oblivious to where I sit by the window-table, sipping at the coffee that they should have served hotter. The window-view extends beyond the pub car-park to a grey sliver of sea. Predictably the day is dominated by thoughts that peep from the shadowlands of memory dating back to the Hotel Eugene Plasky. The older woman is again demonstrably surprised when I draw back my chair and stand to leave. The sandwich is half-eaten, the coffee hardly sipped at. She must be wondering why I bothered to show up a second time. At the till she's compelled to say something, to extend herself beyond her usual abruptness.

Just moved here?

Yes ... renting the lighthouse-cottage.

You'd be a neighbour 'a Pat Finch then.

That's right ... he's been very helpful.

She begins to say something. One can see the workings of her mind in her eyes and on her expression as she agonises over whether to speak or not. She's considering the implications of what she wants to say, weighting up the possible fall-out. It may be nothing more than the latest scrap of village gossip concerning Finch, a crude observation about his interrogations of the heavens with his eight hundred millimetre refractor. She bites on her lower lip, embarrassed by her own hesitation. How many times has it back-fired on her in the past, gossip tail-spinning back into her face? The pub-owner asking for a quiet word out back. She's bitten off the words she'd meant to say to me. I'm an outsider after all, almost certain to misunderstand her true meaning.

A short distance from the pub there's a general shop with a post-office in an annex. A payphone is partially covered by a perplex orb and there's a business directory close by on a shelf. Two customers are talking too intently to the postmistress to notice my presence. I flick quickly to the medical section of the directory and without much trouble find a suitable doctor. I tap the name and number into my phone contacts list and leave directly without bothering to acknowledge the others. Outside I text Corinne, a simple sequence of words to let her know I've contacted a doctor. I'm not lying as I took the time to look the doctor up in the business directory. I looked, connected eye with conscious thoughts and the memory in my phone.

In the following days and nights the hours are absorbed by the sea and the lighthouse. Walks along the

57

headland and communications with Corinne by phone that always seem incomplete are the hub of a simple routine. And the past of course. Always the past.

There's a terseness to Corinne's texts, an agony of pauses in our phone-conversations. She's stopped talking about her friend of a friend post-Kleinian analyst, hardly ever asks when I'm coming home. In the darkness of the lighthouse-cottage nights I try not to think about her so relentlessly as I mine the past for the defining events that led to that crime in the attic-rooms of the Hotel Eugene Plasky.

Pat Finch goes out of his way to point out Perseas in the night-sky, explaining the purpose of the Swift-Tuttle comet. As if I care about what must always be tangential. He sees that too, how miserably I respond to the abstract. Yet he tells me at what given hour one can feast with the bare eye on the illumination of fragmenting perseids.

The final thoughts each night before sleep are always about Corinne, about how I must find a way of getting home to her. On the second night by the coast I woke from a nightmare where I was falling in front of a London tube-train. Passengers waiting on the platform calmly discussed my chances of survival. I woke just before I disappeared beneath the train. Not that any of it matters. Only getting back home matters. The minutes and hours are nothing other than a deliberation on how to get home to Corinne.

In the evening following a turgid afternoon of rain Pat Finch taps on the window facing the sea. It's a shock at first, an intrusion on a bad conscience. But who can it be only Pat Finch. Nobody else knows I'm here. Through the window he goes into a dumb-act, indicating the telescope and the action of looking through it. The skies are clearing and he's excited by the possibilities overhead. I hold up two fingers and mouth the words 'two minutes'. The interior is appallingly empty, with only the phone I've brought from London in any way symbolic of warmth or a connection to what is human. Memory is yielding nothing. There's nothing contained within the remainder of the evening except an emptiness that stretches the entire distance to Greenford.

I'm surprised by my own eagerness to escape the cottage, to be amongst human beings. On the short walk to the Finch's bungalow I'm again stunned by the presence of the sea. Finch is beaming at his front door before I get to knock or ring the bell. His body-language is exuberant. He can't wait to deliver the technical data he's memorized, the exact distances between stars and planets. The skies are clearing, the telescope irrelevant. As he ushers me inside he's explaining how methane decomposes in sunlight as if we're both cosmologists working in a research agency. His two girls are awake, playing a board-game in their pyjamas, bickering quickly, their argument over in seconds. Fruity aromas of cake-filling drifts in from where his wife is baking in the kitchen. She calls out to him. Then she calls out louder to be heard from the other side of the bungalow. She's waiting for him to get around to tackling a chore. But he's too preoccupied to answer, leading me to a side-door.

I've got a fascinating magazine about the planets I must lend you," he says. "Did you know Pluto looks ten times bigger than what it actually is? It has this atmosphere of hydrocarbons that blocks sunlight. They call it a stellar occultation.

I smile weakly, nod as if I'm interested in what he's saying. I don't know what he wants, what he hopes to discover about himself or the world by spending so much time with me. I follow on through the side-door that opens to a yard enclosed by timber garden-fencing. The telescope is mounted centrally, covered by canvas. He unveils it with a flourish and his attempt at a regal bow, allowing me the privilege of a first view. He stands back expansively, gesturing like the king of the cosmos.

They've demoted Pluto from its status as a planet, he says as I press my eye to the lens. They discovered a rock in the Kuiper belt only a few hundred kilometres smaller than Pluto. Now Pluto isn't a planet any more.

What is it then?

I don't know ... a rock in space I suppose.

I crouch to the lens, intrigued by the possibilities of the telescope's power. I ought to be at home in Greenford dealing with the discarded washing-machine dumped in the weeds at the foot of our garden. I ought to be completing jewellery designs for Peter Branwitz to show to the jewellery-house who commissioned them. But yet I'm in Ireland, in the yard of a man I barely know, looking through his telescope as he talks intimately about the phenomena of stellar occultation.

I focus the telescope on a star that probably isn't even there any longer, its light taking a million light-years to reach us. I console myself with the thought that the vast and incomprehensible universe couldn't possibly care about the long-ago sins of one insignificant man. And if there's a creator why should he give a damn about what insignificant men do in the darkest hours of their unformed years?
I

swivel the mount in a sweeping exploration of the stars, wallowing childfully in the glory of space. I can hear Finch's voice, aware the words are not impacting on me. I move from the lens, turn towards him, mindful that I'm his guest and that he doesn't need to take the trouble to show me the stars. He's talking about meterorites, about how more than a ton of them fall to earth each day.

He wants to take out his cosmic charts but I say there isn't time. There'll be other nights for discussion on the progress of comets and asteroids, to search for Orion. I stand back further from the telescope, half-turning towards the door. He can see I'm distracted by the problems that brought me here.

Indoors the girls have vanished, pieces of their board-game scattered on the table. The interior is unimaginative in design, devoid of books or unnecessary detail. He must keep his astronomy charts and manuals locked away in a private compartment, separated from his domestic life.

You have time for a drink?

Not just now.

Sure, I understand...

Another time.

You should drop over next week. Mercury will be at its most visible elongation.

He can see my deficiencies, my preoccupations with less solar matters. His role in fatherhood induces him towards a universally patriarchal outlook. He's easing back on the cosmological observations as he walks me to the door, even though it's hard for him considering all he has to say.

Will you be okay over there by yourself?

I wonder what he means by that, as if there's an alternative to the solitude of the lighthouse-cottage. I'm yawning as I leave his front door, wondering why when I'm facing another night alone Pat Finch comes across as somehow lonelier. I'm an outsider, a London suburbanite with the shortest possible lease on the cottage, but yet Pat Finch can't welcome me enough into his world. He hasn't bothered trying to link together the defining disasters in my life, to probe for the key failures. He's opened the gates to his kingdom of long-socks and knickers drying on radiators, a world of femaleness and temporary escape through the lens of a telescope. He may be searching for the moment when fate consigned him to this life on the peninsula, or the moment it cut me free from Ireland.

We find and shape our own vague roles where he's listening and I'm his informant, passing on facts of growing interest to him. Talking with Pat Finch is a confirmation that mostly life is a series of bit-parts and step-on roles that furnish degrees of information in the lives of others. I've become his guest informant, imparting the required information with a truthful nod of re-assurance, opening gates to other realms by answering questions about my life in London. It's little enough he's asking for – hardly anything at all.

The click of the locking mechanism on the cottage's front door is the loneliest sound I ever remember hearing. The darkness in the seconds before I find the light-switch is enough to make a man yell out in despair. I've dreaded this for decades, the truth of darkness and isolation. Corinne texts to say not to bother ringing, that she's exhausted and gone to bed early. In twenty two years she's never said she's too tired to speak. There's a disconnected element in her words, a sublime but suffocating withdrawal of love. We both know it's because I'm concealing the emotion that brought me here.

The alternative is court-rooms and prison-cells, the procedures of incarceration. I make for the table by the back-window facing the sea. The newspaper cuttings and the chessboard look hopelessly forlorn, the pieces arranged as per the penultimate development in the Korchnoi-Karpov match. Sitting, I resume the mental re-construction of the games they played, then examine the position of the pieces from different angles, hoping for an answer, for a way out of this hell.

Chapter 7

With M. Goudron it was always about the work. Where I lived in Brussels or how I passed my free time didn't interest him. Only punctuality and a worshipful devotion to the studio-hours mattered. A working fanatic, he thrived on the precious metals running through our fingers. A short series of stone steps and a metal door separated the basement workshop from a workshop where three senior craftsmen worked. But both workshops were distinct worlds that rarely collided. M. Goudron isolated me from the others, playing on my formative skills with the exactitude of a master. It would have been unbearable in any other circumstances, but I too was obsessed by the work, offering myself each morning to his will.

Methodically he signed the documents for the completion of the apprenticeship, wrote monthly to the apprenticeship body in Dublin to update them my progress. He overlooked the alcohol on my breath in the mornings, the palmed yawns, signed the residency forms required by a pedantic branch of the Belgian police. He lit panatelas with a gasoline-fuelled silver wick-lighter, smoking in solemnity, as if in ritual. With M. Goudron it was always about the work.

He surprised me one morning by talking about the death of the singer Brel, saying how once he experienced a performance in a Brussels club beneath a single spotlight. I pretended to understand the degree of passion he was trying to describe, made the appropriate facial gestures. But how could someone like the unformed man I was understand or have knowledge of songs about dreams that never came true, about how little happiness there is in the world? Much later I'd have understood the sentiments that brought tears to M. Goudron's eyes as he recalled them. He spoke on about Jacques Brel and I looked away. He spoke about the hope in Brel's songs that whatever happens there's always the pursuit of love and tenderness and the hope that one day we might understand who or what God is. The games in Baguio City dragged into October. In game thirty it looked like a draw from the opening moves onwards. After forty two moves both grandmasters gestured to the officials simultaneously. The game was drawn. The games had already exceeded Allekhine's epic battle with Capablanca in 1927 and against Euwe in 1935. After thirty five games Karpov was leading by five games to four, with twenty one draws.

In the room of dead flies at the Hotel Eugene Plasky I'd began compiling clippings from the London Telegraph and Le Soir. In time it grew into an archive, the quote from the killer Leconte and other thoughts written by hand into the margins of the newspaper cuttings. I must have copied out Leconte's words after what happened in the hotel's attic-rooms. Only at that time could I have had any interest in the words of such a monster.

Using the cuttings from old newspapers, yellowed and brittle with age, I re-create the definite moves of the thirty fifth game on the chess-board by the window. Korchnoi's victory in that game astounded the world of chess, nudging up the score to five victories each with twenty five draws. Playing from white Korchnoi opened with a variation of the Queen's Gambit. Karpov made the wrong decision by pausing for too long before sacrificing his queen for the white queen. After an adjournment Karpov played with the speed of his reputation, his moves completed sixty minutes before Korchnoi. Not that it helped as Korchnoi picked off his pawns at will. I stare at the chess pieces, hoping for new understandings, but see only chess pieces.

It's harder as the days pass to shake off Pat Finch. I've began checking through the window to see if his car is parked up or not before I leave the cottage. It's as if he's been waiting for years for me to get here, to fulfill his expectation for the avuncular neighbour he's always longed for. Before I make it onto the headland he sees me from his kitchen window and hurries away from what he's doing. He knows I've seen him too, knows that the etiquette of the peninsula demands that I wait for him. He's wiping food from his mouth with a tissue, bursting with news.

I've got binoculars for you, he says excitedly. I knew I had them somewhere.

Thanks Pat ... but the birdlife isn't my priority.

He looks at me longer than one would normally expect, one eyebrow arching. He'd heard the excitement in my voice when I mentioned sightings of sandpipers and merlins, worried that already I've lost enthusiasm for the peninsula wildlife. But I'm only worried about how easily he disregards the limits of another man's freedom. It's important not to allow my preoccupations to spill into his life. He's merely living through the kind of days and nights he's always known.

On the headland Finch looks at me in pity, pointing out a spot where the coastguard pulled another body from the sea the previous summer.

He wasn't from around here, he says shaking his head from side to side in sympathy. He bobbed on the sea for days before anyone spotted him.

He might have fallen from the rocks, I say hopefully.

Out of all the strands on the coast it had to wash up here.

There'd have been activity on the water, the coastguard circling. Maybe Finch's family caught a look at the swollen corpse as they lifted it from the water. We stand in reflection, looking towards the spot where they made the discovery, pondering the kind of luck that ends a man's life in the sea. They'd have scooped him from the tides like an exotic form of sea-life that nobody's sure of what to do with.

I guess you heard about the Dagmar Hoff case.

No, I say flatly. Not that I can remember.

It made the main evening news at the time. She was working as an au pair only a few miles from here ... then she disappeared.

I look out to sea, caught up in the dilemmas of my own life. The disappearance of a person I've never known weights lightly on my thoughts.

Did they find the body?

It seemed such a natural question to ask but he pauses far longer than necessary before answering.

She'd popped out to post a letter, he says making a cracking sound with his knuckles. But somewhere between the postbox and home she vanished.

The cracking sound is so alarming that I wonder if he's accidentally broken a bone in his hand. He sees the sound has unsettled me, suddenly unsure of himself, unsure of what to do with his hands. We begin walking slowly along the headland as a dingy with a feeble outboard motor crosses the bay. We pause to watch its pathetic progress until it wheezes out of sight behind rocks jutting out from the peninsula. He sighs, then continues talking.

People always think the worse when someone goes missing. Everyone thought the man she worked for was guilty. They brought him in for questioning more than once. Everyone thought he'd done her in...but they found out that she'd run away on the spur of the moment with some boy she'd met.

And that made it onto the television news?

Probably a quiet day for news … and anyhow, people think the worse. The whole county was out searching for her.

A happy ending at least.

I suppose so … but people around here would have been happier if she'd have been murdered. Give them something to talk about.

There's a quality to Pat Finch that's not simple to pin down, something about his expression when I mention Corinne. He only sees a man alone, cast out from society, womanless. For him there is no wife in London or anywhere else and the only visibly immovable feature of my life is the solitude of the lighthouse-cottage.

In the absence of a body, I say, Or signs of a struggle, why would people assume the worse?

They always do … naturally they thought he raped and murdered her.

His phone rings and he digs it out from a kangaroo pocket in his windcheater. With the absoluteness of a father's love he can't see the disfigurement of a turned-up nose. He can't see his wife's manliness either. In the realm of flesh he travels blind. He'd fall into a slumber every night with the smell of her skin in the dark, each new day binding them closer. He'd find not a second's meaning in a foreign street of whores or the attic-rooms of the Hotel Eugene Plasky.

It's the wife John.

He doesn't have to say anything further. The briefest grimace says what needs to be said. He has to go. His symbiotic reflection needs him. As he jogs back to the bungalow he invites me for a drink in the village that evening, shouting out his words over one shoulder. He's moving quickly so I raise my voice to say sure, that'd be nice. He shouts out the name of the pub and the time he expects to be there, stumbling over rough grass, all caught up in the needs of his wife.

Through a prism formed by Pat Finch's normality the gravity of what lies ahead is unbearable. If I'd have stayed in Ireland, never left my home town, they'd see me how they more or less see each other. Yet by the sea, in the absence of the killing indifference of Central line trains, I feel almost thankful. Here only fundamentals matter, the accumulation of heart-beats, the hope of more life to come.

The leopards' head, the mark of the goldsmith, dates back to the London of 1300. Naturally that city began calling the closer I came to qualifying. Hatton Garden, Regent Street, Goldsmith's Hall – I'd known about them before I'd ever set foot in the city they belong to. It was inevitable I should find myself on its impersonal streets, knocking on certain doors, goldsmithing tools to hand.

At first it was much like the aftermath of any trail of deviancy. At first fear, the anticipation of a knock at the door at an hour when ordinary citizens don't knock at the doors of others. And then hope, the rationalizations of brighter hours, justification peeping from unexpected corners. After Brussels it was natural to assume London held the answers my unformed consciousness had hoped for. After Brussels anything was possible. Unlike Belgium there was no procedure for registering one's address and business with the police. Nobody asked for identification. In the first rooms I rented in Barnet and later Waltham Forest nobody inquired as to how long I planned to stay or why I'd come to London. They must have assumed eventually everyone arrives in London, if they've a reason to or not.

How easy it was to disappear. If I hadn't met Corinne I'd have gone to the end of that road, until I'd disappeared as fully as it's possible in a modern city. As years passed under the loving tutelage of Corinne other problems and ordinary-day dilemmas displaced the residual dread of a day of reckoning. In time I became normal, an industrious goldsmith with reasonable ambitions. In time only my life as witnessed by Corinne held value or quality. Like countless men before me I sacrificed my freedom at the altar of Corinne's love for me. The past faded until it was genuinely hard to tell if I'd really done what I had done, or whether the defining scenes belonged to a film or a novel of influence from the past.

Before Corinne I instinctively lost myself in the impersonality of London's most indifferent areas. So many many more were busy losing themselves at that precise time, forming invisible ghettos of broken individuals starting off for one more chance. Among a circus of guilty secrets my two misdemeanours were hardly worth mentioning. Before Corinne I didn't truly exist, not how legitimate citizens are intended to exist.

My name didn't appear on electoral registers or on doctor's patient-lists. As a freelance goldsmith I practiced the craft where possible, paid for everything in cash. Moved from rented room to rented room in an arc extending geographically from Golders' Green to Leytonstone to East Ham. I joined chess clubs and played at a reasonable level, got drunk at the appropriate times when others were getting drunk. I missed weddings and funerals in Ireland, only just making it home in time to see my mother deteriorating into insanity. Chasms opened up everywhere. Often as I travelled on the underground or walked along yet another busy London street it was if I'd lost my identity as an individual, as if my personality had merged with the anonymous tide of faces that broke in every direction. In the truest sense, before Corinne I simply didn't exist.

Chapter 8

In the Hotel Eugene Plasky Sonia stepped from the communal shower-cubicles on the ground floor wrapped in a white bath-towel. I stood transfixed, as what I was seeing was beyond comprehension. She lowered her eyes, recognising the inadequate who stared at her so forcefully as she passed in and out of the hotel. Apart from a three or four inch scar on one shoulder the skin was unblemished, every pore releasing an intoxication of sexuality, the white towel accentuating her sallow-brown complexion. Wordlessly I watched her pass, turning to see her jog barefoot into the shadows at the end of the corridor.

The chess pieces in the lighthouse-cottage are arranged as per the Pirc Defence opening of the thirty second game of the Korchnoi-Karpov match. Clinically Karpov went to work, brushing aside Korchnoi's brilliance in the preceding games as if they never happened. In the final stages of the game Korchnoi played on even though strategically the game was over. After forty one moves he gestured a defeat. Karpov had taken three months and thirty one games to finally win. We never understand until we've walked down that same road, retracing the steps of others. The post-Kleinian acquaintance of Corinne waiting with a prognosis, eager to offer his perspective, to try and validate all his years of training. Corinne too, convinced by the latest psychobabble. The liberated circles she moves among rarely pause for breath in these matters, the consensus already formed. It'd never be my fault, never that easy. There's proof after all that I'm not a psychopath - the suffering is too intense.

In slack moments through the morning I try to imagine the post-Kleinian friend-of-a-friend's approach. To begin with how could anyone in their right mind take him seriously? But that's just it, an individual seeking him out wouldn't be in his right mind. He'd begin slowly, imposing unnecessary silences, easing into pseudo-Buddhic postures. He'd ask if I'd ever suffered a chronic fatigue illness or health obsession, or if I'd ever indulged in bizarre notions of grandiosity. Then he'd push further into the beast, inquiring if I'd ever been diagnosed with an environmental or parasitic allergy. For one to believe in the cure one must believe in the process.

The absence of the everyday props of home are an endless irritant. The traffic at Greenford roundabout, the familiar signs pointing towards the airport. The hedgerows along our street are lost friends. How intimately they welcomed me home evening after evening, without ever asking for anything in return, a rustle of hellos in the breezes. Here by the sea this life is nothing but an endless process of trying to make it home.

I stare at the chess pieces until I want to smash them to the floor along with the 'Encyclopaedia of Chess Openings'. I'm angry at what I know this is leading to, the events in the attic-rooms of the Hotel Eugene Plasky that can't be brushed aside any longer. I grab the phone, pull on my duffel and rush outside; craving the strands, the unconquerable sea.

The clouds are ominous, a grey-black prediction of rain straddling the horizon. I know Corinne is quietly seething because I ignored the post-Kleinian friend-of-a-friend suggested remedy to all this. She'd love to see me prostrate on his couch, working our way down the box-ticking process until we got to the part where get I filed away in a box marked 'victim of sadistic superego.'

Jemma Finch is driving the girls home from school, just pulling into the bungalow's gravel driveway. They've spotted me, the strange man from the lighthouse-cottage. I look downwards, pretending not to have seen them. I quicken the walking pace, hoping she doesn't beep. I'm escaping another encounter with the Finchs, understanding more acutely that ever that it's just one damned thing from the past that's brought me here. It's always been one damned thing. For some seconds I feel its full weight, imagine what kind of experience that'd be for Corinne. In the middle of one of her hyper-busy days – the call from Greenford police station. Bad news about her husband from an awkward constable, the body waiting to be identified in the mortuary.

Corinne hasn't got a lot of time to think about my mental problems. But when she does have time she always concludes that civilisation is to blame; repression and unconscious guilt manifesting in self-destructive behaviour. She loves me too much to think I actually deserve to suffer. I tried to talk it through with her once or twice but she placed one finger softly to my lips, referring to my unconscious punitive ego as if it was a separate entity that had split away and carried out the filthy deeds single-handedly.

Corinne pointed it out to me first. Or at least pointed in that direction. I'd never very much time to read Freud, or to attempt to superimpose relevant strands of psychological reasoning into my everyday life. I don't think I've ever met anyone with that amount of time on their hands. As an unformed man I was too busy surviving life to seek out the abstract. Later in Greenford I was too busy working long hours and developing my love for Corinne in my free time to actually sit down and read a page or two of psychology. But when she pointed it out, it all made immediate sense. The darkness of that old house I was brought up in faded almost to a shade of light. It was like a veil lifting. I could see for the first time into that nub of the key matters, into the emotional vacuum of our family.

I read the passage over and over, then read it aloud to Corinne. It was all to do with lovers when they are in complete accord with each other, how they don't need the world or anyone in it for their happiness. How they don't even need the child or children they've created through their love.

When I first read through it I wanted to dig out the numbers of my sisters in Australia, to ring them in excitement at the revelation. And to call my brother in Ireland too, hoping he'd speak with me in spite of the practical and emotional distance I cultivated through time. To read out the words over the phone, to explain why we were so unloved, so unnecessary to our parents' lives. But somehow the moment passed quickly.

Why would they not know that, having lived with it every second of their lives? Why would hearing it spoken in succinct terms make them feel any better? Maybe knowing that eminent figures in psychology focused the fiercest of intellects on the phenomena might have comforted them. I gave up the search for my siblings' phone numbers almost as soon as I began it. Then put away the Freudian textbook, hoping that I'd never again have to re-visit its pages.

Lovelessness is just that, lost opportunities for intimacy or communication. What's lost is lost forever. Impressive contextualisations by great thinkers don't help. Once must only work it over and over in the comfort of one's mind to grasp that fact. The sadness and loss fades in time, like everything fades. In time even the lovelessness of children or parents is forgotten.

The sky is grey, dense and overwhelming, oppressing the coast and all hopes of sun between now and dusk. The light plays shadows on the headland, altering it so that it resembles no known world. Rain is already falling, colder than rain is meant to be; a water-therapy for the weary. It'd be futile to walk into the intensifying rain so I turn back. If I was thinking normally it'd be no trouble to find the number of the car-hire firm I used to find the lighthouse-cottage. A vehicle would free me from the mercy of the weather. That is if I was thinking normally.

In the depressing light of a late afternoon burdened by a deluge the lights from the windows of the Finch bungalow are touching reminders of home. There's no easy way out of this, no simple route back to Greenford. I pick a black pawn from the chess-board, hold it in the palm of one hand. The Korchnoi-Karpov match had nothing to do with chess – how could it? In the solitude of the lighthouse it's a very simple trick to slip past the distraction of chess. During the Korchnoi-Karpov match my father lay dying in an Irish midlands' hospital. I'd ring from the phone in M. Goudron's office, listening to my mother crying. She said he wasn't the same man, that they couldn't sit him up in bed, that he didn't recognise his own family.

I promised I'd make it home to see him before he died, to hold his head in my arms regardless of the coldness between us. We hadn't fallen out as such, but hadn't bonded in the first place as father and son. A drunken uncle at a family funeral years later said my father privately believed I was the son of a popular priest whom my father was convinced had a brief affair with my mother. Not that such things didn't happen. But I always thought that wasn't the problem, always thought my father simply hated all his children, not just me. I don't know why he bothered fathering us, but he did. Our mother tried at least, tried to overcome her boredom at having to dedicate time to children. She defended him to the end, said that he wasn't always that way, that through time something happened in his mind. Either way I didn't show up for the funeral, let alone the deathbed rites.

In Brussels I must have done the same as what I'm doing now, running through the sequences that lead home, even though there was nothing there to return to.

Home then was that draughty, dark house on a slow hill in a town lost in the Irish midlands. The flight to Dublin airport and then waiting despondently at the luggage-carousel for a suitcase with nothing of use inside. Going through the motions as one is expected to do. The bus ride to the centre of Dublin and then a short walk along the quay or down Talbot Street towards Busarus. Looking at other people being happy, leading gregarious lives. The scenes of gradual progress towards home, the abruptness of dialect, the same man at the same street-corner shouting for the Evening Herald.

On the bus journey from Dublin there'd have been the usual wave of sadness, an unmerciful depression descending. The business of a city fading into the vivid greens and browns of the midlands. By the time the bus passed into the town's square I'd be sunk hopelessly again in the familiar torpor. The great mind-healers of the world tend to forget that one sparkling panacea for depression, the one-way ticket from the complacent towns so many of us know.

And then from the town square down a long lane of stone cottages, the elders staring unforgivingly at the very few who pass. The emotions of the young or the outsider hated far more than concepts of devils. On pass the houses of what were the middle-classes, until the slow hill appeared between the broken stone walls of a derelict eleventh century abbey and chestnut trees forever circled by disturbed crows. Before I'd have made it to that old house with the leaking gutters and wild garden it would have been impossible to go on.

Impossible too to face a hospital ward and a mother's tears, a loveless father propped up unseeing on pillows. I turn the heating stat to max, run a bath and soak in it until I feel almost human again. As I'm drying off the phone rings. Naturally I think its Corinne but it isn't. It's Pat Finch, ringing to say he's running twenty minutes late. I'd forgotten we'd arranged to meet. I can't remember sharing my private telephone number with him.

I sleep a dead sleep for a half an hour, waking without thinking I'm back in Greenford like I'm prone to do here by the sea, knowing in my bones I am where I am. The rains have faded to almost nothing but there's an unseasonal darkness to the day. I ring a taxi firm operating from the village and the controller promises a car in ten minutes.

The controller knows who I am, knows where I'm travelling from. After such an expanse of years in somewhere as impersonal as London it feels invasive to have someone outside my intimate circle knowing about my existence.

From the lighthouse-cottage to the village the taxi-driver barely speaks, hardly much beyond a word or two about the weather. He doesn't ask me where I'm from or what I hope to find by the sea. He drops me off cheerlessly, waving to a couple passing on foot, ignoring the final words of thanks I say to him. I've disappeared in my own country, existing as a taxi-fare or a stranger standing at a bar-counter. I don't know what else I expected. Only the inanimate is welcoming, the obdurate presence of the lighthouse, mothering waves from the sea.

Finch is as late as he said he'd be, bringing the latest news. A fisherman's skiff was spotted off Raven Head, overturned and without signs of life. He's wearing a sports' jacket that's too tight at the chest and shoulders, red blotches on the nose and cheeks that look like the beginnings of rosacea.

A minke whale washed up on the peninsula, he says as we make our way to the counter. And two sea-anglers not from around here thought they'd come across a large seal. Can you believe that, a large seal!

The sea has merged so fully with his personality that it's hard to imagine him as a separate entity. At the counter they're talking about politics, a surge of words from several directions in the verbal shorthand of newspaper headlines.

We've had all manner of carcasses washing up around here, Finch says proudly. Human remains too. You'd never know what the tide might land in on top of you.

He introduces me to two men drinking solemnity in one corner. Finch wants them to like me, grinning idiotically. He describes them as Bargy men as if that's supposed to be of significance, small-holding farmers from Forth Mountain, dismissing me after a grunt and a briefly raised glass. They turn their ballooning forms away, return to monosyllabic exchanges.

We're due soon for a partial lunar eclipse, says Finch turning from the two bores.

He didn't miss a beat, used to it by now. He pretends he fits in as much as the others, but anyone can see he doesn't. He'd be almost a novelty in the village pubs, his free hours claimed by family and the lens of his telescope. He pitches his words as if he belongs to the inner-sanctum but even a stranger like me can see how they keep him at bay, indulge him like men speaking to a boy. There's a spiral of carefree moments between the second and third whisky. Finch is crowding the counter, insistent on fitting in.

One of the drinkers from further along the bar rushes to the toilets, vomit leaking from fingers clasped to his lips. It's a fragment from my father's Ireland, a night of dry-hawkes and cigarette-smoke.

I wasn't born on the peninsula, Finch is saying as he leans into my ear. I'm from a townland not far from here, where the Bann meets the Slaney. A truly lovely part of the country...

It's a perfect waste of an evening, listening to foolish talk about where Finch took his first-ever steps, the revelations of male inadequacy. Finch is disturbed by his phone as he talks sentimentally about the fields and rivers of his boyhood. It's his wife calling. His expression is troubled by a half-terrified look seen on men's faces when they're worrying about money or scrambling in their minds for the right words to say to their wives. When he pockets the phone he doesn't have to say anything, his face says it for him. He must leave, hurry home to his wife. I make it easy for him, say that of course he must go, that we can meet any other evening. One of the girls is running a temperature, he says in apology.

He hurries off, his family only minutes away, their lives wholly conjoined. For some moments I'm envious of him. I've never before strayed this far from Corinne, never imagined I was capable of straying this far. Worse than this separation from Corinne is the knowledge that nothing has shifted, that there's so much more in the way of getting back home than a simple itinerary. I don't know what I was expecting, what powers I imagined the sea to have. At the counter, in Finch's absence, I try to look normal. They don't need to know about this crisis; what's private is just that. Even if it means the ending of a man's life. Waiting in London are the same trains and stations, the real likelihood of a step out of this world from a Central line platform.

Chapter 9

The night descends emphatically as if intending to stick around far longer than the morning. All traces of starlight are blocked by a phalanx of low cloud, the lighthouse-cottage interior lifeless, without animation or purpose. Now I'm more orientated the neglect is obvious; hiking boots caked in mud from the gleys, a pattern of mud walked into the floor from the front door to the back-room. A prominent tuft of mud flecked by grass is propped by one of the table legs. Damp stains the hallway and unused bedroom, traces of deathwatch beetle in the sapwood doorframes. On the first day I experienced only the ideal sanctuary, not noticing the chemical smell as if the previous occupant had tried to treat the dry-rot in the ceiling beams. Fungus like blackened toadstool dot the bathroom walls. I'm seeing the squalor of the lighthouse-cottage in a loop between my only other experience of true squalor, that room at the Hotel Eugene Plasky.

I'd tucked it all away neatly, the humiliations of an unformed man in the Brussels of another decade. Those humiliations meant nothing because they belonged to an earlier, stranger manifestation of the man I am. The face on the underground train in London was vaguely familiar at first. But only vaguely. At first I thought it was a face from the world of jewellery design, a buyer perhaps I'd met at one of the meetings Peter Branwitz manipulated me into attending. I hardly any notice, just a second glance. The carriage was crowded even though it wasn't rush-hour, so I moved slightly from where I was standing for a better look. I thought that on a third glance the name or place might come to me, the jewellery house associated with the oddly familiar face in the crowded train-carriage. Then in seconds the full impact of what I was looking at hit me. The face had naturally changed with age but I was certain it was the face I feared most. It belonged to another decade, to a hotel of despair and pain in a time of darkness. But yet I was looking at it among a gallery of ordinary faces on the London underground, trying to fathom its meaning. Almost directly the headaches began.

The conversation with Corinne that night started late and ends early the next morning. From the beginning her tone is terse. She says she needs to talk, to purge herself of impulses that relate to both of us, and that I need to listen. There's a leak in the bathroom and one of the cats is staying out at night. A transaction at a bank requires my signature along with hers. She needs to share the details of our life in Greenford, like we've always done. She needs to say these things.

My head's clearing, I say. I'll be home soon.

She wants me to spell it out in blood over the phone, re-assure her again and more convincingly that it's nothing to do with her, nothing directly to do with our relationship as man and wife. I try to describe the lighthouse-cottage, omitting the evidence of structural decay that I didn't even notice until so recently. She says the school inspectors can go to hell, that she can make it on a flight from Heathrow first thing tomorrow. She's already checked the flight schedule. There's a pause after she says that. And by allowing the pause to filter through her intuition she knows I don't want her to come here.

Inevitably very soon after that pause the tears begin. I can't decide if she's crying about the state I'm in or about her failure to make everything right for me as she always makes everything right for me. Or if she's crying about a matter that's got nothing to do with me. I hold the phone away from my ear, unable to bear hearing her like that. She's coming apart, maybe just as much as I'm coming apart.

You haven't rang Peter Branwitz.

I'll ring him tomorrow.

The designs...

I said I'll ring him tomorrow.

She's quietly angry too, the distance between us as disconcerting as a night-intruder in the bedroom. We're both perturbed at why we're not having this conversation in our bed in Greenford. That's where I'm meant to be. We read each other's pauses. In the background one of our cats is miaowing. I know which one it is, know that she needs Corinne to know that the bedroom door is closed and she wants to get out, or that she's hungry or thirsty. I listen beyond Corinne's words, to the window of our bedroom as it rattles a little in the night-winds.

Please ... don't cry.

I'm not crying.

She's lying. I can hear the tears down the phone. She's not snivelling, making the usual crying sounds, but I can hear the progress of her tears down her face. For several minutes after we ended the conversation I just sit quietly, incapable of movement. We'd spoken right through midnight and in the waking hours of the morning. We'd paused more times in the conversation that in any other conversation we've ever had. She knows there's something fundamentally wrong above and beyond the stress of London. I can't hide the truth from her because she reads the pauses between my words too accurately. But I can't come out and say it, not in a clear choice of words.

I sleep without bothering to undress on the divan in the room dominated by the lighthouse, just about mustering the energy to kick off the filthy hiking-boots. I've ran through in my mind at least a hundred ways of telling Corinne what the problem really is, but no matter how it's dressed up it's not plausible. She wouldn't believe me anyhow, wouldn't believe I was ever capable of doing what I did. She's got too much faith in me, our destinies fused as one for far too long.

I wake well into the next morning with a psychic pain, near noon, a fear as broad as the coast itself. Gulls scream on the headland and someone's knocking on the front door of the cottage. The metal flap of the letterbox cracks for a second and then a third time. From the sanctity of semi-somnolence I climb into the new day just as whoever's banging on the door begins shouting in the letterbox. In the sleep-sedated thoughts of morning I can only think of a tide warning, the sea breaching the headland.

When I get to the front of the house there's no one there. Whoever knocked has gone. Then from the window of the unused bedroom I see Pat Finch reaching for the handle of his front door. What exactly does the man want? I'm an ice-hearted bastard, an atheist angry with others as much as towards concepts like universal love or a brotherhood of man. If there is a universal emotion it must be hatred. Other than Corinne and the cats every relationship I have is functional. They use me as I use them. There's nothing else to it – no hidden depths or subtext written by a sentimentalist with academic tenure. There's just an intimate circle, a way of existing as a human being in the world. Everything else is hatred and contempt. That's how it is, even though I'm tore apart inside by what happened in the past. And in the absence of a convenient witch-doctor with the appropriate spell there's no other way to turn.

Out on the headland the sea again takes me by surprise. If there is a god it must be the sea, or a phenomenon born from the sea. Nothing else shows its power so effortlessly. Nothing else dissipates the paranoia so mercifully. There's a shout from the direction of Finch's bungalow. He's standing in front of his car waving, holding a cloth in one hand like as if he's just wiped down the windscreen. I want to walk on, nonchalant, content in my own routine, to ignore the conventions ofbackward little villages. But before I've time to analyze things further I'm walking towards him.

He feels sorry for me, even though he's the loneliest-looking man I've come across so far in life. I should be feeling sorry for him, trapped in a cage he's made with his own two hands.

John,he says happily. You're going somewhere?

No... just taking the air.

I can drive you wherever you need to go. Just ask. Anytime.

If he knew why I'm here, the nature of the events in the past I'm trying to pin down with memory. If he could peel briefly through skull-bone and membrane into this mind-life I inhabit. If he really knew me he wouldn't offer his telescope as a mode of inquiry into the cosmos, wouldn't invite me into the snug of his family life.

Thanks, I say. But I'll be fine. I talk to my wife a lot on the phone. She'll come here soon.

I'm not sure why I said that but Pat Finch is happy I did. His inner-life manifests so naturally through his expressions and demeanour that they are readable from quite a distance off.

You're not so busy you haven't time for a coffee, he says.

I follow on meekly as Finch leads the way to the front of his bungalow; accepting that fate has brought me here to this pacified husband and father, this fundamentally lonely man. It's the same fate that led me to that hill of rain and tram-lines in Brussels all those years ago. And to the attic-rooms of the Hotel Eugene Plasky. It's a simple law once understood, like gravity or the temporal nature of flesh. To contest it or reign against it is futile.

Above all else the bungalow's interior is witness to Finch's love for his wife and children. His individual personally is absent in the decor and the photographs on the wall. He exists within the home only as part of the family, smiling coyly from a monochrome shot taken with his wife and the girls when they were much younger. As if to state a point a large colour photograph of the girl with the turned-up nose at about the age of two dominates one wall. They've merged all four of their identities into one single unity, the family portraits radiating a pride in each other. I'm conscious of the filthy hiking boots, the damp duffel I'm wearing that's beginning to smell. Generally I'm a mess. Don't worry about the mud on the floor, he says as if reading my thoughts. It's easily cleaned up.

As he prepares instant coffee he spills sugar on the table, laughs about it, then turns clumsily towards the fridge.

Your daughter, I say ... how is she?

She's fine, he says looking surprised I remembered.

Last night she went to bed early with a temperature. And this morning she was up like a lark, mad for school. And to top it all she seen a porpoise in the sea.

She said it was a sure sign that something wonderful was meant to happen today.

I almost ask if it's the girl with the turned-up nose before remembering it's more a deformity than a characteristic. It's the differentiating feature in his girls, but one that can't be mentioned. He really ought to be sleeping off the strain of the previous night's shift but instead he's fussing over coffee and biscuits for a man he barely knows, ripping open a packet of digestives with his teeth.

It's a slow start to the day, I say smothering a yawn with one hand. I was up very late last night on the phone to Corinne.

He doesn't respond, just looks at me slyly. He'd never make it in politics or poker, not with how he constantly betrays all his emotions and thoughts through his expressions. He doesn't believe there's a wife in London losing sleep over whatever foolishness I'm getting up to. He hasn't asked one question about Corinne or what she's doing in Greenford. He's heard from somewhere that the delusional ought not to be encouraged. When he does ask about my life in London it's in the abstract. How many miles do I live from the Hubble Telescope or do I see any famous faces from the world of television out and about? There's an element to his questions about London that suggest he'd liked to have spent time there, to get to know it intimately. He's sacrificed everything for the coast after all.

Then without any warning he's jumping up and pointing towards the living-room. He's enjoying all this, the fun and games with the quietly tormented neighbour who's washed up on his doorstep. Normally he'd only be so excited about a dead minke whale or the sea-ravaged carcass of an otter. Laughing he hurries out through the hallway, pleased with himself. That's a more obvious fact than the sea itself, that he's pleased with himself. The ambience of the interior is suffused with the females in his life. Not just in the evidence of family photographs and dainty touches like the toe of a pink gum-boot protruding from under an armchair. This is their world, as intimately a part of them as their skin-texture or their last thoughts before sleep. The smells are all female, the colours, the arrangement of objects. Sitting here even briefly one can understand Finch's eagerness to reach out from his female nest. He's back quickly with a whole new series of grins, holding out a package of processed prints. He sits and then pushes the plate of digestives towards my end of the table.

What 'til you see this.

Like a card-sharp he plucks the snaps from their jacket-holder and spreads them on the table. I look from the snaps to Finch's grin and then back to the snaps again, waiting for a clue as to what should happen next. They are the unpretentious exposures of the family beach-holiday. Finch bare-chested, belly rounded like a foal, nose and arms sunburnt. In the next shot a child is squealing high on his shoulders. Then there's a badly-taken panoramic of a fertile coast. He stands abruptly, moves around to where I'm sitting.

They're from last year's holiday, he says. Portugal.

I lean back, uncomfortable with how closely he's standing. He's pointing out a distant rooftop in one of the wide-angle shots.

That's the hotel where we stayed.

The Algarve?

The Algarve, he says happily.

I smell his humanity, as he selects one particular photograph from the wedge of images, man-sweat and the taint of industrial cleaning gel. It's another unimaginatively-taken landscape, a hill with trees bunching at the top, a blotch of grey to one side that might be the sea or a road. He places it beside my coffee mug.

Take your time. Study it.

Mercifully he shifts his bulk from my shoulder back to where he was sitting on the other side of the table. He looks at me smugly, head tilted foolishly to one side. I don't know what to say to him. It's nothing more than a bad holiday-shot, lacking in imagination or composition. It's rubbish - just the ordinary kind of rubbish that clogs up most people's lives. It even lacks sentimental value as it carries no human, no family member or passing local caught forever in innocence or surprise. I look at him blankly.

Look again. Look at the sky.

I pick the holiday-snap up, hold it so that it catches the optimum light in the room. Examine it for some further moments. Then I hand it across the table.

Sorry ... I can't see anything but sky.

He's on his feet again, superbly dynamic within the confines of an interior. He rummages among a display of china before taking a magnifying glass from a hiding place on one of the kitchen shelves, places the holiday snap on the kitchen table, holds the glass a few inches above it. With a nod and an expression the span of a second he offers me the view through the glass. I can't help thinking of our house in Greenford, how everything is double-locked, no short-cuts taken with security. The jealous protection of the hours free from work are designed to avoid a moment like this – caught up in another man's pedantic musings on the trivia in his life.

Again I examine the holiday photo, this time through the magnifying glass. I'm concentrating on the sky, but there's nothing to see but a blur of cloud on the horizon. There's a tiny blot too that looks like a flaw in the developing process. I'm humouring him, waiting for the joke to come. He points out the inconsequential blot, then looks at me with the intensity of a stare.

So what do you think it is?

Looks like a film-processing flaw.

No look closer. You can see it with the glass.

Magnified, his fingernail is filthy and chipped, the finger-tip of a man who sweats and grunts through the working days. He's pressing down hard as he points out what he wishes me to see, as if intent on leaving the perfect finger-print. I hold up a hand in submission.

Sorry. I can't see it.

You can't see it?

No I can't. The only thing I can see is a printing blot.

It's a UFO ... I thought that was obvious.

He's looking at me intently, looking at the holiday snap, then looking at me again. He seriously believes he's seen an unexplained phenomenon in the skies on last year's package holiday. His finger is still pressing on the photo.

I don't want to make a big deal of it, but if you look again closely you'll see it.

I lean back in the chair, far enough from the magnifying glass and the holiday snap so that Finch can see I've had enough of his foolishness. It's a speck in the sky on a poorly-taken holiday snap but he insists it's a UFO. He reads my expression, my last thoughts on the matter. Then he places the magnifying glass back on the shelf, wordlessly slips the holiday snap back into the package of images. He's serious about it, actually thinks he's captured an unknown flying ship on film. And he's hurt I haven't humoured him, that I'm not sharing in the awe of the mysterious. He can't hide any emotion. Everything is written on his face far more effectively than words. As he sits he reaches for the biscuits, embarrassed, searching about in his thoughts for something else to talk about. His hair is a mess as usual, cut wildly. I have to speak, to rescue both of us from the embarrassment.

The church in the village is very quiet.

During the week sure ... it'd be quiet.

They had the gate locked.

He's looking at me over the rim of the coffee mug, crunching a biscuit. Eyes widening as he wipes crumbs from his chin with his free hand.

That's how it's gone ... locks on everything.

Since arriving by the sea nothing tastes how it ought to taste. Not just Finch's weak coffee or the food from the village pubs, but everything. The malaise just has to be internal, taste-buds contaminated by guilt, by a malignant flowering of memory. Finch's coffee tastes more like rain-water, or watered-down chicory. Nothing will taste the same until this is resolved.

The church is losing its status."

You can say that again, he says shaking his head from side to side.

The churches used to be always open."

I can find out the times of the masses if you like.

I stopped going a long time ago.

That's often the way.

He's still sore about the holiday snap, the non-event in the skies over Portugal. For the first time he's stepping back rather than forward. I'm having second thoughts, thinking I should have concurred for the sake of Pat Finch's fragile self-esteem. It need only have taken half a minute to look closer at the processing flaw and to agree that yes of course it's clearly a kind of spacecraft. He's been staring into the night-skies for so long that the sharp edge of his objective view is not as sharp as it ought to be, duller than his other faculties. I wonder has he yet succumbed to the concept of cosmic activity as an influence on human behaviour - the astrology syndrome.

In London I wanted to speak to someone about a personal problem. But, when you think about it ... who is there to speak to these days?

Wouldn't that depend on the problem?

Psychiatry is too abstract. What is it really but a strand of medicine ... and medicine is based on biology and chemistry. None of that really matters ... Wouldn't you say it's more about communication?

I haven't thought that much about it.

He's still surly; a condemnatory gaze fixing on the jacket of holiday snaps on the table between us. He's a sulker, a keeper of hurts and silences. I drink some of the coffee he's made even though it's vile. For a moment I consider bringing up the question of the processing flaw in the holiday snap that he believes has meaning. But time is precious and we can never truly predict with confidence how much of it remains.

Do you think the stars and planets influence us?

You mean like astrology?

Just like astrology.

I don't know. I don't think so. I just know about the astronomy side of it. When I use the telescope at night I forget about everything ... stress, what might happen tomorrow ... all that kind of stuff.

He's allowing the holiday photos to rest between on the table like another trigger of guilt, further evidence of what I've omitted to do. Since all this began practically everything inevitably swings around to the question of guilt in one or other of its forms. He slurps disgustingly from his mug just before speaking.

Do you think if a person was looking for the answer to an important question, they've come to a place like this?

Perhaps ... the sea is an inspiration.

The hurt is leaving him, the rejection he experienced when I didn't collude in his fantasy about the holiday snap. It may have been the only point of interest he felt he had to show me today, in the absence of washed-up carcasses and spectacular events in the sky. Physically he's unwinding, tension in his shoulders lessening, torso slumping forward. He's almost back to normal when he speaks.

Do you have an interest in the church?

What kind of interest?

You know ... when you said the church in the village is locked.

I was just curious.

There's no one else to talk to around here for miles. And the people I've met in the village are uniformly unpleasant and sly. It'd be simply impossible to have a conversation of meaning with any of them. Probably the one man on the peninsula with the humanity to converse on an honest level is Pat Finch. And I've come to practically live on his doorstep. It's the touch of fate again, finding me as it found me so easily in the past. In less than another minute Pat Finch is himself again, relaxed and quick to smile.

I spend so much time looking at the stars I know there's something out there ... something lonely.

I stopped believing a long time ago. My wife's an atheist...

Quickly he's on his feet, rinsing his mug at the kitchen-sink, cheerfully asking if I'd like more coffee. I wonder why exactly I'm here by the sea, what exactly fate wants me to understand. I'm listening out for the prompt with my entire being, for a word or reference that to contextualize this impasse. He stands at the sink washing mugs, talking over one shoulder.

I heard London's a bad place for astronomy. Too much light.

That's right. Mostly the skies are invisible.

That's bad. If you take away the stars from a man's life and you take away a lot.

It wouldn't have sacrificed much by way of principle to agree with him, to concur that yes in all likelihood it was probably a UFO he captured inadvertently on the frame of a roll of thirty five millimetre film. Nothing else could have happened on that holiday, apart from a grazed knee or insect bite. What possible harm would it have caused to have indulged him in the harmless game where he claims to have seen a UFO? Just by our existence as conscious entities we cause unwitting hurt. He turns back towards the kitchen, finishing at the sink, drying his hands in the front of his sweat-shirt.

Aoife practically lives for the pony club, he says.

I think of Corinne back home in Greenford, childless, perpetually busy, without the stars as comfort. The gulls scream past Finch's bungalow, reminding us of our proximity to their world. Finch sits again, pushing the plate of digestives even closer towards me, saying I've barely touched my coffee. I lift the mug, feeling with my lips how the coffee has lost its heat.

Confession is a good thing. Jemma goes regularly. But I stopped going ... ran out of things to say. If I'd have stayed within the fold ... I'd have liked to have confessed. We have a young curate, very approachable. Everyone loves him.

A man must believe, for it to work.

He's about to speak when his house-phone rings. He has much to do. This is his life and I'm here in the midst of it. He rushes from the kitchen to the living-room, answering the phone and then leaving it off the hook. Then he rushes to one of the bedrooms, looking for a number he's written in his address-book. The caller is waiting on the line. Earlier Pat Finch mentioned he'd a shift later that day, his working clothes to organise. I'm up and ready to go, thanking him for everything.

The next clear night you should drop over. The telescope will take your mind off things.

I leave quickly, not wishing to take any more of his time. In the absence of anywhere else to go I make for the lighthouse-cottage. Lies have become a matter of life and death, the normally harmless lies that pepper most people's lives. Corinne knows I'm not lying as such, just skating as close as I dare to outright lies.

Usually the process of ringing Peter Branwitz is easy as checking my phone for voicemails or texting Corinne to tell her I'm running late. In the months prior to leaving London I'd come as close to Branwitz as any man I've known. Almost like brothers. Then in what he must see as betrayal I abandoned the project just when he needed my input the most. Little wonder it's so hard to ring him. Impossible to ring him, to mentally compose what it is I wish to say to him.

Back at the lighthouse-cottage it's all I can think about, Peter Branwitz and why I'm so scared of ringing him - the fear of having to tell more lies. The human conscience can only take so much. When I seen him last on that London underground platform he rested a hand on my arm momentarily. Looked directly into my eyes like how a man looks into a woman's eyes. It was odd to be touched so intimately by a man, a beery smell from his mouth in my face. He went to the trouble of altering the tone of his voice, lower into a baritone bass. He looked and sounded ridiculous, as if he'd copied a pose from a film he'd seen on t.v the night before. A stream of tourists flowed past only inches away, oblivious to the theatricality of Peter Branwitz's gesture.

That problem you mentioned. Is it still troubling you?

Yes, it is.

I just want you to know that you can talk to me. Any time.

Thanks Peter.

I've seen a lot in my time you know. I wasn't always in jewellery.

I inched away from him uncomfortably, never having seen him like that before. It sounded phoney coming from a man like Peter Branwitz. He was never intended to sound sincere in the daylight hours, to be taken seriously as a moral prop. We were both embarrassed at having to dedicate our departure for that day to the gentler emotions. He'd have despised me for giving into weaker impulses by blurting out a stream of nonsensical angst; disintegrating just as we were meant to be presenting a united front to the jewellery house.

It ought to be the easiest thing in the world to pick up the phone and ring Peter Branwitz. What's hard about that? In the quiet of the lighthouse-cottage there'd be no distractions, nothing to get in the way of a frank discussion about the designs. Nothing could be easier. But nothing is more fearful. The phone is a tool with which another lie might be constructed. That's why it's impossible to dial Peter Branwitz's number, or to even look for longer than a second or two in the direction of the phone. The fear of another lie intensifies until I have to switch the phone off. Without a connection to the outside world there's only the night, vague radio voices, and the awesome sea. Beyond all that the burn of conscience. And hope too, hope that it's not too late.

Chapter 10

Often it was nothing but a glimpse of black lace disappearing around a corner, feeding the beast on sightings of Sonia as she hurried in and out of the Hotel Eugene Plasky. Marco imparted adroitly-worded scraps as he lapped up the need. What was one so weak and stupid doing in his world? An unformed man talking to a man like him about a woman like Sonia. He'd nod approvingly as the obsession with Sonia got out of control. Human weakness pleased him; the more vulnerable the weakness, the more it pleased him. He'd say just enough to keep me hanging on, waiting like a fool at the reception desk for further words about Sonia. Two Romanies slashed each other with blades, he said in the last week of Sonia's life. Fighting over her outside the South Station.

I understand why they'd do that, I said.

One man slit from throat to gut.

He must have died.

No, he lived. But he wished he died, because he couldn't have her ... she was already gone.

To wear stitches on the flesh, a badge of love wounded, accepting the knife trauma and surgery with empty shrugs - the purpose of some men's lives. Transfused blood in their veins, the pain of not having her. Did they prowl the streets afterwards in the hope of finding her, passing strangers like me who also hoped to sight her? Marco administered the details lovingly, how when she was younger an Antwerp diamond-dealer swore he'd kill his own wife if he had to, if Sonia said the word. He'd have done anything to have her.

I'd wait by the reception desk each evening after the hours in the Goudron studio, hungry for news of Sonia. Marco spoke gently, as if worried about scaring me away. Sonia is completely free, he'd say. And I give you permission to talk with her any time you like.

Teeth stained and gold-capped. A half-moon scar on his lower-lip hypnotic in how it moved in synch with his words. If he'd have asked me to steal from the Goudron studio I probably would have, or to do worse. I'd have done it, if I was capable of doing it. Nodding and pursing his lips like a sympathetic family doctor. He understood – didn't consider the obsession strange. He totally accepted my weakness for Sonia, because above all others he knew the feelings she provoked in men. With sensitivity, he'd bring a chair out from the night-porter's cubicle so that we could sit together by the reception desk in the evenings. We'd talk of chess or jewellery, but often said nothing. With the gravitas of a master of human frailty he'd nod further understandings. He didn't have to verbalise it. I knew he understood my condition. Much later, if I'd have ever mentioned him to Corinne, she'd have said I must been looking for the kindness absent in every word ever addressed to me by my father. Hoping for surrogate moments of consolation. Or she'd think I'd made him up, that a creature like him could never really exist.

In between bites of andouillette or rognon blancs that he ate cold from a plastic jar he'd ask about Dublin, his questions never too intrusive. The other guests came and went glumly, as if staying at the Hotel Eugene

Plasky was more a sufferance than a necessity, a perverse pilgrimage in honour of a secular or underworld god or goddess. They'd nod briefly as they collected keys, warily looking over one shoulder, parting with minimal words. I sat passively by one side of the reception desk like a docile hotel pet, waiting patiently for Sonia.

Marco offered titbits of cold food or indifferent wine, regarding me with a look of complete sympathy, a prisoner shackled by my own nature. She'd ignore me, always in a hurry, often frantic. Women generally ignored me then, so I expected it. Once or twice she smiled at me from pity. It was never anything other than that. She rarely smiled at anyone, mostly only pausing for the quickest word with Marco. By then it hardly mattered, the obsession flowering in all its malignance. By then I just needed the fix of seeing her, even for a second or two. That freed me to carry on with the squalid routines of what remained of the day.

Most Sundays a private guest called for Marco, with high, bulbous cheekbones and deaths-head tattoos on the back of each hand. The fingers of one hand were tattooed too, with what looked like symbols from ancient text. He'd wait in the foyer, eyes flitting like a lizard from the hotel's main entrance to a door that led to a ground-floor corridor. He never smiled, instead offering the impression that he'd already died and endured eternities in purgatory, only returning to visit revenge on some poor bastard in the environs. When the Sunday visitor called, others intuitively checked if he cast a shadow or not, or if his image reflected in mirrors. The sight of him ought to have done it. But instead of leaving the hotel, I stayed. That's the true crime. Not the actual obsession with Sonia, but that I stayed when there was no true obstacle to leaving.

In the last week of Sonia's life Marco's friend with the tattooed fingers hung about for no apparent reason in the corridor just outside my room. It was impossible to sleep knowing he was around. It wasn't just that his eyes looked all wrong, or the inscriptions on his fingers in black. It was a matter independent of his physical appearance, as if the air underwent a chemical alteration. On first looking back I simply put it down to the imagination of an unformed man burdened by obsession. But analysing it further, thinking it through under the influence of the lighthouse, it's obvious that the air physically changed whenever Marco's Sunday visitor was around. If it was cold, when tattooed-fingers showed up it became clammy. If it was warm, it chilled. On one Sunday I stepped on a dead rat in the corridor, its head missing. Tattooed-fingers had stood for some time in that same corridor, earlier that day, cleaning his fingernails with a clasp-knife.

Summer had almost passed, its remnants dispersed by the colder evening winds along Porte de Hal. With less heat to feed on the drains at the back of the hotel stank less than before. It was just another lifeless night at Marco's hotel. The building creaked and the mice moved beneath the bed. The guest in the room further along the corridor moaned as he did most nights, but apart from that it was quiet. I couldn't sleep, turning endlessly from side to side. I must have thought about Sonia, or why Ginni had walked and out of my life with such brevity, without a word of explanation.

The noise didn't wake me as I was already fully awake in the darkness of a sleepless night. It came from directly outside the room, an uncertain noise that didn't belong to the hotel's backbeat. Climbing quickly from the comfortless bed I paused by the door, ear pressed to the keyhole. It was a muffled, dragging kind of sound. Carefully I pushed the creaking door open an inch or two, squinting into the bad light of the corridor. Tattooed-fingers grunted over a dead-weight wrapped in matting or carpet. Daring to open the door a touch further I saw the night-porter also present, both men dragging the concealed weight through the almost-airless corridor. I closed the door on the inch-wide gap, fearful that tattooed-fingers might look without warning over one shoulder.

They staggered with the strain of the weight until they got to the back-door of the hotel. The door opened, then closed. Then silence. Or the relative silence of the Hotel Eugene Plasky at night. The moaning from further along the corridor, the mice more daring as the hours passed, doors banging from the higher floors. In the morning when I woke it was difficult to know if the incident in the corridor had happened in real life or in a realm of dreams.

Days later I passed the night-porter as he flicked through a magazine at the reception desk. It must have been around nine or ten, close to the beginning of his night-shift. It wouldn't have been any later as I wouldn't have approached him in the hours that belonged wholly to his watch. He disliked me, hated when I hung around the foyer anywhere close to his shift. He tossed the magazine onto the reception desk, frowning and then sneering. The image on the cover was of a woman naked from the waist down, buttocks reddened in strips as she leaned forward. Behind the bending woman a man stood partially in shadows, cane in hand. He looked from the magazine to where I was standing.

So you're still here, he said.

You mean still here in Belgium?

Don't get smart or I won't unlock your lock.

I haven't locked myself out.

Then what the fuck do you want?

The semi-paralysed geriatric who sometimes slopped a dirty mop along the hotel corridors said it wasn't anything personal. It was just that the night porter didn't like people. Foreigners, Belgians, it didn't matter. Everyone has their phobia, said the old man with the mop. With him it was just people. I guess in hindsight that makes sense. Where else for him but the night-foyer of the Hotel Eugene Plasky? I stood back as far as possible as I spoke, not wanting to bug him unnecessarily.

I'm worried about the moaning, I said.

What moaning?

The guy who moans just a couple of doors down from me.

He pays for the room. He can do what he like in it.

He looked at the cover of the magazine again, then looked at me with more hatred than before. Then he snapped up the magazine and stashed it in a drawer in the desk. He banged the drawer shut and stared at me as if it was my fault that he needed to buy books like that.

The guy must be in a lot of pain, I said.

What do you want me to do about it?

He ought to be in hospital.

Okay. You take him to hospital.

Before I'd a chance to answer he jumped up from the desk, a disgusted bantamweight smelling of toilets and stale cigarettes. He didn't have to say it. I could see it. Marco's night-porter was angry enough to kill.

Why are you here?

I just wanted to tell you about the moaning guy.

He didn't know what to do. Already he'd worked himself to the heights of anger. There wasn't anywhere to go from there, not without him doing something radical. He edged back from the desk, backing against the wall, trapped by his own rage. I took a step back too, speaking as calmly as possible.

Marco said when he's not here I should speak to you ... if I have any problems.

The storm had mostly passed through him. The mention of Marco's name contextualising our relationship. Whatever about the night-porter's phobias Marco's shadow fell across every unclean corner of the hotel. And he knew Marco was my protector, nurturing me until the day I'd be of use to him.

You shouldn't involve yourself with other guests, he said.

The moaning keeps me awake.

You shouldn't be here.

I'm here. We can both see that.

His face twisted as if he'd just had a minor stroke, back pressed against the foyer wall as if an invisible force had pushed him there. He looked terrified, as if he'd just taken an air injection into a vein and was waiting for it to hit his heart. I looked over my shoulder to check if someone else had entered the foyer, but we were alone.

Shaking, he pulled back the chair he'd been sitting on as if ready to sit again. Seeing the fear in his eyes I knew Marco must have forced him to work at the reception desk as a punishment. There's no way he'd have volunteered, not a freak like him. Marco knows all about that man, he said lowering himself into the seat.

Soon he'll leave here.

You're saying there's nothing you can do?

He had to get rid of it, to alleviate the weight of disquiet transfixing him to the spot. He'd have said practically anything to see me walking out of the foyer.

Marco doesn't like people talking about his private guests, he said. But if I tell you about that man will you leave me in peace? Will you go back to your room and promise not to bother me again?

I promise.

He lightened visibly, knowing I'd soon be out of his face. And if he timed it right he might not have to see any other guests for the remainder of the shift. Replenished the toilet-rolls and putting the bins out back at strategic times.

That man can't see or hear," he said. Brain-damaged too. That's why he moans.

What happened to him?

A woman poisoned him with anti-freeze. His liver and kidneys messed up too. Soon Marco will take him to a nursing home. Just don't go telling everyone what I said.

You haven't said much.

Leave it! That's all you need to know.

Something had obviously happened to him, one of those unexpected, traumatic events that change people's lives. Or a lengthy linkage of degradations with no known cure. It couldn't have just been his nature. The damage hung in bags under his eyes. He'd just about come down from the pitch of rage when I spoke again, knowing what I had to say would send him up there again. At that point the sound of my voice alone might have done just that.

I saw you in the back corridor, dragging a heavy weight. You were with Marco's friend.

What else did you see?

Nothing.

You sure of that?

Back on his feet again the energy in his eyes and demeanour changed. A damaged and fundamentally ineffectual man, forced by a foible, a weakness or a debt, to work the night-shift in Marco's hotel. What mistake led him into that lair? I held up both hands in an expression of innocence. Naturally he thought I'd seen more than I actually had.

Why do you stick your nose into the hotel's business?

I just want to help. The next time I wouldn't mind helping you out.

If you want to help then get out of here. Leave and never come back!

He banged open the night-porter's cubicle then banged it almost immediately shut. In the circumstances even the dullest could easily comprehend the preamble to murder, his bare hands to reaching out towards my throat. That's what he really wanted to do, choke me into lifelessness instead of attending begrudgingly to the hotel's filthy corridors. He grabbed a plastic bucket from beneath the reception desk, hurrying from the foyer, giving me one final evil look as he went.

He'd have saved me if only I allowed him. To yield just once to his words, that would have done it. Nothing complex or difficult, to just take the advice of a man who hated me but who understood the workings of the Hotel Eugene Plasky more than most. He couldn't tolerate my physical presence, yet he was willing to save me. Get out of the hotel as quickly as possible. He couldn't have said it more clearly or with more urgency. But by then thoughts of Sonia had taken over the rational side of my mind. Impressions of her were all I lived for. I couldn't hear what the night porter was saying, or what others were saying. Or willingly didn't hear what they were saying.

A nod to fate, just like what happened on that hill of rain and tram-lines was a nod to fate. Ignoring that warning. Fate was present on that evening in the hotel foyer as he spat out the words. There wasn't any easy way around it. Nothing to do but stay until the very end, until fate opened another door.

Under a spell from the lighthouse and the sea images from the Hotel Eugene Plasky begin to form with startling mental clarity. Growling sea-tides and seagull-screams hardly interrupt the waking dream of reflection, the flow of memory gifted by the coastal repose. The hotel foyer floor, filth in the tile-joins; the corridor of the moaning guest and then the door that led to that room of squalor. The melancholic harpist Kathleen Ni Houlihan among the images on the Irish stamps and franking marks from my home town that accumulated by the bed. The letters were all unanswered, disjointed sentences and incomprehensible references a precursor of my mother's decline into insanity.

First, short confinements of a week or so. And then the final twenty three years of her life in a specially-built annex of the regional hospital. Her boney fingers entwined rosary beads, dribbling and rocking on a chair by her bed. On our last visit she gripped Corinne's wrist as she leaned over to wipe her chin. The ferocity of the grip surprised both of us. That was the last time we seen her, shrivelled to half her size, sitting up in bed. Staring but not seeing, confusing her imminent death with the advent of her honeymoon sixty years before. Corinne wanted to arrange another visit that year, but we didn't get around to it. In truth I couldn't bear any more of it.

The unanswered letters by the side of that bed in Marco's hotel have followed me all this distance to the sea, picking at fresh guilt-scabs. Among that pile of letters terse lines from my brother, inked from a suppressed anger. Harsh words and threats of disinheritance, even he knew I wanted nothing from the sale of our old house, nothing from that town or anyone in it. Through the years, usually, around the time of a wedding or funeral, he'd want to know why I never stayed in touch. He couldn't fathom that, the retreat into silence. When he wrote to me that time in Brussels I must have read his letter in bed, stuffing it back into the envelope and dropping it among the other unanswered letters. Then staring again at the cracks in the ceiling I'd have carried on obsessing about Sonia.

My brother knew more than anyone that it was useless talking about it, that it wasn't worth a postal stamp or the laziest composition of written paragraphs. As the older one he'd have felt compelled to say something, to assume the older sibling's role of authority. He asked the wrong question of the wrong person. By the time we were born it was too late. The questions were unasked long before that. There'd have been an element of choice surely. I mean nobody would have physically forced our parents to bring children into the world. In their case having children wasn't a celebration of their love for each other but a socially-imposed adjunct to it. By the time we were gifted with rational thought that house on the hill of respectability had become silent and tense, a house of departure. Sisters bound for Melbourne, the embarrassment of goodbyes.

In a dusty drawer in the spare room of our house in Greenford there'd be yet more fading letters; a sister's invite to Australia. Unconvincing, couched in terms of duty or guilt. The ordinary kind of guilt that people pick up like germs from public toilets. Corinne always said she'd never understand the lack of warmth or intimacy in the family I come from, the extremes people go to in avoiding each other.

The following evening after the incident with the night porter at reception a slop of greenish liquid spilled from an open door as I walked along the ground-floor corridor. It drenched my shoes, the toes of the broken brogues immediately discolouring. I looked up in surprise, directly into the night porter's face. He'd been removing stains from the room with an acidic solution and accidently spilled it from a bucket. We looked down as the chemicals popped and bubbled on the shoe-leather. Just then he seemed to lose a degree or two of his hatred for me. Maybe he was worried about the solution burning through to flesh and then a complaint to Marco.

I reassured him, said the cleaning product hadn't burnt to skin. He was almost civil as he assessed the spillage, cursing his own carelessness. He picked up the overturned bucket, locking the door of the room he'd been cleaning. His clumsiness was opportune as I needed to ask him a question. Out of all the people in Brussels I had contact with a man as fundamentally malevolent as that hotel night porter was a natural choice. If anyone would know about a violent death in the locality it'd have been him.

That guy who went under a tram near the North Station, I said. Did you hear what happened?

No ... I didn't hear what happened.

They're not sure if it was accidental.

He looked like he wanted to express himself, but he reigned it in. If he hadn't spilled the chemicals he'd have simply cursed me. But he held it in. Later I dumped the shoes in the hotel's garbage-chute. Over the course of an hour or so the chemicals had eaten through the leather. Just as I returned to the room of dead flies I heard the night porter's voice again. Crouching by the darkened room doorway I spied through the slimmest gap between door and door-frame, wondering why Marco and the night porter had

118

showed up in that part of the hotel. Business-like they used a master-key to let themselves into the room of the moaning guest. About a minute later they emerged in a shuffle of bodies, supporting the moaning man by holding one arm apiece. He tried to speak, rolling his head, but only another pained moan materialised on his lips. From the angle of the slightly-opened door the moaning man's profile was visible for only a matter of seconds.

The eyes were fishy and staring, clearly sightless; shocked and disorientated, but above all angry. It didn't really look like a human face, more like a face from a totem-pole, cursed and frozen in stone or timber. Marco and the night porter bent their heads slightly towards the man in a gesture of concern. The solemn party inched slowly out of sight in the direction of the hotel foyer. The image of the moaning man's face was impossible to shake off, like a subterranean catch perpetually hooked and gutted. The caring stoop of the night porter, Marco's soothing words. In the light of his story what person wouldn't pity him? A victim of his own nature, another statistic ruined by a woman. The unseeing eyes stared as if injected by a sadist with a toxin. That part of the hotel was empty without the moaning man, the corridor linking with the reception area. The quietness rested sullenly at night. Though I'd never actually spoken to him, I missed the moaning man when he went.

If the night porter hadn't heard about the incident on that hill of rain and tram-lines then I began doubting if it had really happened. He lived off the misery of others, wouldn't have missed a death almost on our doorstep. Lying awake at night I deconstructed my recall abilities, the actual events of the night. The tram cut him cleanly in two. The human mind couldn't conjure that out of nothing.

It was late, the cafes of Ixcelles closing. He'd cracked her hard in the face. She fell with arms and legs flailing. He spat at her as she lay there groaning, walked on with a swagger. The hill was dark; rain, tram-lines, the streets mostly empty. I followed on, not knowing why, ignoring the hurt woman lying on the cobbles. At a point on the hill the darkness was so intense I could just make out the man's form ahead as he cursed to himself. I felt nothing, no anger or compassion, nor sympathy for the woman, nothing. The last tram of the night loomed like a metallic monster, bearing down on us. When it levelled to where he paused to light a cigarette I'd already stepped into the shadows of the building next to him. I pushed him hard at the base of the spine before he'd time to inhale from his cigarette, exactly at the right moment. He disappeared beneath the tram and I turned in the direction of the squalid room, anonymous in the night, deeply satisfied with how the night had turned out.

Curiosity not guilt kept me awake back then; waiting for signs of tattooed-fingers in the hotel corridors. Wondering why the night porter said he hadn't heard of the man's death under the last tram from North station. He'd have been the first person in Brussels to have known about it. He'd have made it his business to know about it. I'd stare harder at the cracked ceiling of the squalid room, turning it over and over. Then it was impossible to see it simply as a question of murder or of a thoughtless son ignoring a dying father. It didn't matter why fate had used me on that hill of rain and tram-lines. It was just a question of surviving the fundamental workings of an unformed consciousness.

Throughout the days and nights that followed I rehearsed in my mind what to say to the murder police when they showed up. The narrative varied in detail every time I ran it through it. In the most truthful version I admitted stumbling into him in the dark, but that I'd nothing against the man, didn't know him from Adam. It wasn't my will that caused his death, but rather a presence in the night. People often call it 'fate' for want of a better word. Personally, I'd very little to do with it. I guessed the murder police wouldn't be pleased by that line of answering, looking on impassively as a maggot tried to wriggle off the hook. I'd have liked to have said it anyhow. But they never asked, because they never came looking for me.

After work in the Goudron studio ended for the day I'd hang around the hill where it happened. Retracing the dead man's steps, checking to see if they'd cleaned away all the blood and gore, trying to remember where exactly the woman he hit had fallen. Wondering too if she'd have appreciated the impulsiveness as a tribute to her honour. I was looking for evidence that it had really happened, that fate had used me so dispassionately.

The route of the last tram from North Station passed the cafe at the very top of the hill that night. Unpretentious, its facade neglected, the obligatory drunk propped at the counter like an object left behind from the night before. I'd walk up the hill after work, following the run of the tram-lines to that cafe. I'd order a beer and stand among a row of malcontents at the counter.

The same customers looked at each other with the same contempt, before continuing with their solemn drinking. The cafe manager looked tired of them all, perhaps tired of life too. With quick gestures of fingers and thumbs he'd indicate he'd seen and heard it all before. Or he'd sit beneath a television screen stroking his grey goatee thoughtfully. On the few evenings I went there I was the only one of the counter sober enough to verbalise an entire sentence. For that fact alone he was happy to listen to me.

I heard there was an accident on the hill, I said.

You mean the tram accident?

I heard the guy jumped.

Who can say? The tram-driver saw nothing.

He wasn't suspicious. I didn't look impressive enough to be anything other than an inadequate foreigner. It was just conversation, talking about the accident on the hill or the politics of that day or how Anderlecht got on in the football. It meant nothing to him either way.

Was he from around here?

From Liege I think.

What a pity.

People should be more careful when they go out at night.

In cafes like that logic doesn't follow the expected model; questions answered out of sequence, the conversation overlapping. Just after talking about the train accident on the hill the cafe-manager answered another question from further along the counter. The bar-talk had a natural rhythm. It wasn't the time to probe, to dig for further gems about the incident. They couldn't have divulged any more anyhow. They all heard it was an accident. What more could anyone say about it?

After a dreary hour in the cafe-bar I'd walk down the hill to where it happened, pausing where the stranger from Liege had died. Fate had taken his life. I'd only played a minor part that night, the role of an underling, nothing so important to merit remembering. They didn't write about it in the papers, nobody mentioned the death. It wasn't personal. His blood was splashed on fate's doorstep.

The nights in the hotel that followed the incident on the hill of rain and tram-lines were more degraded than before, more unread letters from home heaping by the bed, telephone calls to my mother deferred indefinitely. Other than the working days in the Goudron studio there was little to live for. The Korchnoi-Karpov games were more and more abstract. I drifted in and out of the building without a true presence or centre of gravity. The marks of decay in the hotel were reminders of the death-scene playing out in a hospital in our home town. But by then the death of my father was as abstract as chess. I'd forgotten about Ginni and how she'd disappeared so abruptly. The whores on Rue d'Aerschot lost whatever interest they might have had. In longsight a crime of that magnitude can never be qualified, even if certain factors leading to it fall loosely into the realm of human understanding. Isolation and immaturity. The first pressure of desire intruding like a tumour on a critical function of the brain. The intense longing of seeing her in passing in the hotel foyer. By then only Sonia mattered.

The chipped, flaking paintwork ended at the stairway leading to the hotel's attic-rooms. Beyond that point the interiors were tenderly painted and cared for, the lighting more subtle and optimistic. Brass roman numerals identified each ornately-panelled door and honey-rose incense burned. The attic-rooms belonged to Marco and his private guests. Nobody else dared to go near that part of the building. It didn't need a warning sign or an impediment that had to be scaled or unlocked. The tightly-spiralled stairway communicated all that was necessary to communicate. The uninvited didn't venture past that point.

The steps leading to the attic-rooms amplified the concept of sound. Tiny sounds outside the scope of the human ear intruded on reason, the movement of cockroaches, the web-weaving of spiders. I tip-toed up the first few steps, so that my head was level with the tight corridor dissecting the attic-rooms. Low, sleepy music came from behind one of the ornate doors, so low that at first it was hard to identify it as music. A male voice increased in volume from inside one of the attic-rooms. Hoarse and vulgar voice, unmistakably Belgium, asking questions of one who remained silent. The voice escalated to a growling bass, ugly and slow like a voice taped and then played at the wrong speed.

The door of one of the rooms clicked, a hand operated it from within. Someone was about to exit the attic-room. I spun on one foot, disappearing from the spiral steps, running along corridors and down stairways until I made it to the sanctuary of my squalid room. The hotel was sunk into disquiet, the mood abnormal but nobody wished to talk about it. The old wreck who sometimes mopped down a hallway or landing said he knew nothing, just laughed and said everything was fine. The night porter couldn't speak to me about it even if he wanted to, not with his hatred. Around then, just as I dared take a tentative step on the stairway leading to the attic-rooms, I should have packed and quietly left that place forever. There's no excusing it; not then, not now. I stayed when I should have simply went. And because of that I'm here now by the sea, when I should be at home in Greenford.

The next evening Sonia dashed through the hotel foyer, running as if in the chase of her life. I'd been sitting on the front step of the hotel indolently facing out onto an empty street, tired of living, head hanging between my knees. She didn't notice me, or if she did she looked through me as she always did. I meant nothing to her, my life pathetic and meaningless. If I'd sat on that step for the remainder of that year still I couldn't think of any reason why I should mean anything to her. I turned to follow her. I knew where she was going, where she always went. I almost dropped the idea of following her at the foot of the steps leading to the attic-rooms. Fear, only because of fear. I'd no business in that part of the building. If the night porter or Marco saw me on those steps I knew I'd be in trouble. There'd be no excuses, no way of laughing it off. I imagined what they'd say if they did see me, the sudden change of expressions. So carefully I backed off, I hurried along the corridors and stairways to my room. I stretched out on the bed for an hour, maybe two hours, eyes running back and forth over the crazy moonscape of the cracked ceiling, the desire to see Sonia pressing on the inside of my skull like a living, malignant entity.

Nothing interrupted the flow of idiotic thoughts. If it had, then none of this need have happened. I'd be in Greenford idling in the back-garden, occupied with the mundane, or on my way to another meeting with Peter Branwitz to do with the designs. This couldn't exist, even in the form of an idea, this business of trying to save my life here by the sea. Nothing impinged on the obsession with Sonia. Holy medals blessed by saintly hands that my mother had sent me were disposed of by then. The dry, detached logic of great thinkers in several second-hand paperbacks collected from junk shops and the flea market at Rue Blaes were as useless as the bodies of the shrivelling flies in the hotel room. Nothing saved me, not logic or the simples of a mother's faith. Alone and free, I weighted up the only one thought worthy of occupying such moments.

Just like that night of rain where the tram-lines scarred that hill a force outside the physical pushed me on. What kind of defence is that? What judge could bear listening to it for even a minute? If civilisation is based on logic then to offer a defence like that is to insult logic. There is no defence, not within the borders of reason. Yet for what it's worth there was a force outside of me pushing me on. Not that it makes much sense, or in the light of other happenings even matters.

In stockinged feet I crept back to Marco's lair, this time not hesitating on the spiral steps. I edged on towards the one door in the attic-rooms that was open. The music I heard earlier had ended, and the slow voice silent. Instead I heard an uneasy breathing, a kind of female moaning. The room door was opened several inches and I paused directly outside it, straining to hear. It sounded just like a child or a female struggling for breath. Quietly I pushed the door, then stepped inside. I knew the rooms had to be small and that whoever was inside would see me immediately, but I went ahead with it anyhow.

Sonia lay tied to a four-poster bed, draped in red velvet. She was stretched so that her legs pointed in the direction of the door, semi-conscious or sleeping, head slewing from one side to the other. Someone had tied her hands above her head and she was naked apart from a black silk slip. Her eyelids were shut but opened a once or twice for a second or two to show only the whites of her eyes. The slip only just covered the breasts and pubic hair. Nothing else came into focus only Sonia, lying there with her wrists tied to the bed-posts, framed by velvet.

Was it seconds or minutes? I don't know how long I stared. Concepts of time were meaningless. Every isolated moment of fear and doubt I'd known in Brussels culminated in that vision. It was inevitable, something I had to see. There was no other possible way. I heard a brief noise behind, turned to see Marco standing passively in the doorway. He wasn't angry, as he wasn't a man to hide his anger. If anything he was mildly surprised, no more than that.

You must be looking for me, he said.

No... not really.

Then you came to see Sonia.

I can't get her out of my mind.

He placed one hand paternally on my shoulder, his calmness genuine and steadying. Gently, without an emphasis of contact, he guided me towards where she lay. We looked down at her sympathetically, like close relatives at the bedside of the gravely ill.

I understand, he said.

I wish he hadn't understood, wish he'd lashed out with one of his brutal hands, pinned me to the nearest wall. It was because Marco understood there was no way of stepping back from the check-mate involving the three of us. With Marco's hand on my shoulder, his breathing controlled, there wasn't any human way of stepping back.

Chapter 11

Jemma Finch is out jogging on the strand, hair tied back into a pony-tail. Her sweat-suit is surprisingly tight, two red blotches on either cheek like the first touches of a circus clown's make-up. As she jogs closer I see the sheen of sweat on her forehead. She smiles, waves; a quirky, feminine flurry of one hand. I try not to look at the phenomenal bounce, but it's impossible. She must notice the direction of my stare. How many occasions she'd have seen that look, on the beach or in the swimming pool, or in summer sun as she innocently undoes the top button on her blouse. The true shock is the pert protuberances of the nipples through the fabric of her top. She's braless.

I don't know what to say, or if it's appropriate for a man in my situation to say anything. I can't take my eyes from the shape her breasts create beneath her sweat-top, even though she can see I'm staring. They're not sagging as breasts of that size often do. Exceptionally large but firm too, sculpted by nature to a Rubenesque distraction. She calls out cheerfully, a mention of the weather. I'm hoping she stops but she continues on jogging. Why would she stop anyhow, interrupt her morning routine to be gaped at? I watch her go, turning a full one hundred and eighty degrees without having any reason to do so. Her behind is formed by the firmest curves of true womanhood too. The tightness of the sweat-suit reveals Jemma Finch in a whole new light, as if she's unzipped herself from an oppressive and uncomplimentary skin. I grasp new understandings of the husband in this vision of the wife. Her powerful arms and shoulders mean nothing, an irrelevance in the context of how she looks in her sweat-suit. I whistle softly in admiration through my teeth, too softly for her to hear.

I continue walking in the direction of the village, reflecting in the long view on Jemma Finch. My original perception on the first days by the sea was skewed. Nothing is more obvious when considered within the reality of how she looks as she jogged by. As if seeing it for the very first time I see the mystery of womanhood unveiled in her very presence. I didn't see it at first, perception clouded by the misery of my own predicament. But now it's obvious. I see it, understand it fully. Nothing other than the presence of the sea itself is more apparent. Only a pedant or a man without interest in women couldn't but see it that Jemma Finch is beautiful.

The gulls are swooping on coarse sand and shingle, picking about in a sea-spit on the mud-flats. In a freer world it'd be conceivable to stretch out among the bracken and wild pansy by the sand-dunes; to lie indolently, unseen, unremarked upon, until the next rain or storm-tide. There's a shorter route to the village by a shingle beach with a border of reeds. But it'd be easy to slip on lichen by a lagoon formed by seawater seepage; an oozing blackish sediment. I stick to the coastal trail of hardened mud.

The image of Jemma Finch out jogging stays with me for the entire distance to the village, a reminder just in case I've forgotten about the needs of men, about our fundamental dilemma. It's puzzling to think that the woman I see hurrying from the family saloon to the front door of her bungalow is the same woman I've just seen out jogging. Instead of fear and guilt or concern as to how all this will end, suddenly I'm only thinking about the symmetry of figures. It must be the isolation of this scenario, the loneliness elevating the desirability of Jemma Finch above all else.

In thinking about the female figure it's only expected the next sequence of thoughts are not far from Corinne. In the months before I left London she complained about her vaginal flora. The way she just came out and said it made it sound like she'd a garden growing up there. There'd been other problems too; an uncomfortable dryness, oestrogen cream always handy by the bed. She'd looked the word up on the net, dyspareunia. Sex had become near impossible, the penetration too painful for her. I try to remember the exact date it is today and manage to pin it down to within a day or two. She'd be due for her mammogram soon. We'd spoken about it very briefly on the night before I left. She'd been reading a magazine article about how childless women are more prone to breast cancer, worried because she'd never an infant on her breasts. I wonder would Corinne find anything of meaning to say to a woman like Jemma Finch? Worlds separate them but perhaps they'd find a connection if they had to, a strand of sympathy that always appears mysterious to male eyes. The intrusion of sexuality on the peninsula is surprising, bringing with it a new dimension of vulnerability. The sight of Jemma Finch in her jog-suit, nipples straining under stretched fabric, is changing the entire coast. If sex can penetrate this far up the peninsula, then it surely has no boundaries.

A seagull swoops close overhead, catching me by surprise so that I duck in fright. There's no obvious food in sight so the creature must be diving in a territorial gesture. Gulls screech along the headland in frenzies, caught up in their own aviary logic. Common terns skim a reef of rocks, limpets and barnacles. A solitary horseman canters on the strand. Oyster-pickers have abandoned their trestles on the lapping shoreline. Kelp is tideswept on bedrock. 'Deadman fingers' plants cling to the side of boulders. A large-bore pipe lies broken in the silt of a sea-leak by the dunes. In these same skies the mute swans of summer flew by not long ago, migrating to the wintering grounds of other shores. Gulls must be nesting eggs nearby as they are swooping unusually low, an instinct in all nature. I think of Corinne childless, nothing for her to protect with the human version of graceful diving swoops, except the cats perhaps. For the first time in what must be years I think of Jamie. It's a natural progression of thinking, from the gulls protective of their young to Corinne, and then to Jamie. I don't know why I didn't think of him earlier. How easily he slips from my mind. Children were never a priority for Corinne. In natural terms we had problems anyhow. We'd have discussed it, the possibility of fertility clinics. But it was low on the list of our concerns. We were saving for that house in Greenford at the time, both of our careers devouring most of our energies. We'd never convinced each other that we had space in our lives for a child. And besides, Corinne indulged her mothering instincts on the cats. Personally, having seen what I'd seen of families growing up in that Irish midland town I was against the idea of children on principle. But I'd have gone along with it for Corinne's sake. I didn't argue the point, left it entirely to her. I had everything I needed in Corinne. Anything other than what we shared would have only taken from us, not added to us.

It never came up seriously in conversation for years, but then out of nowhere Corinne wanted to foster.

Again I didn't argue or contest the point. Although the more I thought about it the more hassle it seemed. She began speaking about it all the time. Late in the evening, by telephone, she'd speak to her friends about it. I must have thought of my own father and how utterly useless he was as a parent, how he died with only our mother's tears to comfort him. Never having known a father's love, how could I give a father's love? But for the sake of Corinne I'd have tried. One morning in the kitchen, after breakfast, she threw her arms around my neck, crying about the prospect of a child in our lives.

The questions and assessments intruded on all aspects of our lives. We jumped through one bureaucratic process after another, filling in form after form, attending meetings facilitated by overly-serious young women from social services. Throughout the whole process I could see it meant the world to Corinne. Who was I to stand in the way of her happiness?

It was an act of secular contrition that ground its way forward for the best part of a year. We never balked at any question, no matter how invasive. We made no complaint, purged ourselves of so much selfishness in the process of offering ourselves to the state as suitable candidates. It took a long time, an interrogation over many months, but then Jamie appeared at our house in Greenford, frowning at the kitchen table.

It must have gotten to her through the years, friends talking about their children. Baby talk in the staff room, the business of child-rearing discussed. She's spent all her working life among children, so people must have wondered how she'd slipped free of motherhood. Sometimes I'd watch her silently as she read or listened to music on headphones. How supremely fulfilled she looked, content and complete within the structures of her own existence. She didn't need other people to achieve personal attainment. I'd wonder if she really needed me.

During the fostering assessment she was totally driven. I'd never seen that side of her before. She didn't rest until every last section in every form was completed thoroughly. Maybe she felt guilty too and that's what she was trying to do, purge herself of the guilt-demons of imagined sins or misdemeanours. How can one truly say what goes on in the minds of others anyhow?

It was a mistake from the very beginning, from the first minutes of little Jamie's time among us. I looked searchingly at Corinne; she looked at me. We knew without exchanging a single we'd done the wrong thing. After a few days Corinne made the necessary phone-calls and Jamie returned to where he came from. Two female social workers showed up in a taxi one morning to pick him up. They were terse and quietly angry, contemptuous of us as human beings. They hardly spoke to us. Corinne signed a form they'd brought with them and that was that. We never spoke about it after that morning. The matter of our childlessness never came up again. We were cured by Jamie's brief stay in our lives, released from another imposition of need.

A Little Egret postures in the tide-borne silt of the strand, intensely vulnerable; a yellow-toed, frowning genius of the air. The coast gives so unexpectedly, unasked-for gifts that can't be repaid directly, this day or any day. As the coastal trail of hardened mud ends a roundabout marks the beginning of the village, cars feeding it from off-shooting roads. The village's only street is lined on both sides by parked cars. I think of Pat Finch's words, 'no car, no legs'.

The locals look at me more pointedly, most likely alarmed at the mud on my clothes, at the state I've allowed myself to get into. It might just be my imagination but they look at me a second or two longer than before, as if they've discovered a degree of irrationality or nonconformity in my eyes that went unnoticed before.

They're not surprised to see me in the pubs so early in the day; no raised eyebrows or frowns. At least they understand that particular weakness. There's several in the midst of a drinking session already. The runt with the hole in the sleeve of his plastic jacket is at the counter, head slewing to one side. He's in a mess, as if he never made it home last night. Or if he's slept in the back seats of a friend's vehicle in the pub car-park. He looks right through me, nothing registering. He's either too drunk or too tired to argue.

I claim a newspaper discarded on one of the chairs. It's from yesterday but that hardly matters. I browse through it, mildly interested in news from around the world - the coverage of rugby union games. The barman lingers longer than necessary before asking me what I'm drinking. It's hard to say if it's personal or if he's just absorbed in his own private dilemmas, trying to work out if a woman or other really loves him. He says something in a rough voice to the runt that I don't quite catch. It's a day for drink. People sense it beforehand, a drought that begins at the throat and stretches back to an earlier year. Bar-workers see it coming too, see the signs before an actual drink is lifted.

Engrossed with the newspaper crossword puzzle an hour passes quickly, and then another hour. I doubt if anyone noticed I wasn't merely drinking whisky and working on a crossword puzzle. I doubt they'd have noticed I was fighting for my life. When nobody is expecting it the runt at the counter falls sideways, clipping the top of his head off a bar-stool. A few regulars curse him spontaneously, but without malice and the barman mutters about previous warnings. They've all been through it before, much like workers tiring of a weekly fire-drill. The barman dries his hands in a cloth thoroughly, without any sense of hurry, and then leaves the sanctuary of his pumps with a steady purpose to his movements. Without sentiment he and one of his regulars lift the groaning runt upwards. With firmer grips he's guided towards the door and in seconds is out in the street, words of wisdom from the regular shouted after him whether he needs them or not. If they noticed the blood trickling down one side of his head they never mentioned it. I leave soon afterwards. Not because of the incident with the runt but from a sense of personal decorum, a sense of preserving boundaries. In the pub directly next door the smaller of the two bars is empty.

In the wider drinking space on the other side of the serving area a young couple with an infant are feeding coins in turn to two gaming machines. People notice solitary drinkers, so it's always best to use more than one pub. That's the only wisdom I remember my father passing on. Not that he cared much for human beings or whether they drank alone or not. It's just sometimes when he drank he shared his store of drinking advice,

136

or advice on money. If there's a selfish gene I've inherited it from him.

I've tried to re-construct in my mind the hours that followed those drinks in that second village pub but there's nothing but a haze. What could have happened in a deserted village pub on a mid-week afternoon? If anything did happen I've little or no memory of it. The last time I drank like that was during that apprentice year in Brussels, the whisky on that night hitting my throat like water. I was barely even aware of it flowing into my system.

There's only one memory of those missing hours, painful and regretful. I must have rung Corinne, or she rung me. The conversation was brief, fractious. She almost definitely hung up, her tolerance for whisky-words limited.

It was the stars and the sea-winds that tempted me towards the short-cut back to the cottage. I stumbled over a dune, scrambled up and then stumbled again. The sea-air must have revived me as I remember more of that uncertain walk than any of the previous hours. The ground was dangerous in the dark, so inevitably I fell again, more heavily the second time. I shouted out in rage, not at the darkness of the night or at the treachery of the broken ground but at my own stupidity for thinking I'd gotten away with it. The earth underfoot closed in on me yet again, the silty-black sea forming puddles in the wet strand. In the distance the lighthouse beamed out majestically to the night, dignifying all human concerns by its very existence. Then I guess I must have passed out.

I wake with brownish-green spots in front of my eyes, under a strange ceiling that dances and shimmies alarmingly. The blackening patches of damp overhead are familiar, but I can't work where I've seen them before. The sounds of gulls screaming by the window are reassuring, an indication that I'm still alive at least and somewhere near the sea. I turn through a spasm of pain that emanates from both the base of the skull and the stomach, easing into a position on one side where it's possible to sleep. Voices whisper at the foot of the bed but I can't physically sit up to see who they belong to. The moments of consciousness are unburdened by guilt, that simple gift is appreciated above all else. Very soon I'm drifting into a delicious sleep.

I wake with a headache and an urgent need for the bathroom. As I sit upright and swing my legs towards the floor I freeze with pain. The fresh wave of pain manifests at a point behind the eyes, shooting out vindictively to my four limbs. I curl up like a baby and after a full minute of taking the pain full-on am ready to try and complete the exercise. When I finally stand upright I realise why the ceiling looks familiar. I'm in the unused bedroom of the lighthouse-cottage. I make it stiffly to the bathroom, sick with hangover pains, bent over to ease the worse of one particular jab of pain, lightly touching an aching lump on one side of my head.

I realise my duffel, cords and sweater are missing. And even more surprisingly, that someone's mopped the cottage floors. My hiking boots are scrapped clean and resting on a folded sheet of newspaper on the bathroom floor. In my underwear I scoop cold tap-water onto my face and neck. Without knowing what day it is I hurry back to bed, lacking the required energy to hunt for aspirin.

It has the quality and weightlessness of a dream but it's not a dream. The first sensation is the lavender from the soap she uses. I've noticed it before. On this side of the peninsula it could only mean only one person. Jemma Finch is leaning over me, punching a pillow into shape. She touches my shoulder and I'm smiling before I open my eyes, my psyche invaded by pleasure. She looks as concerned, as if she's at the sick-bed of one of her children.

You're awake.

I think so.

Do you need anything?

I'm not sure.

I smell her breath she's so close; a warm breath of peppermint and camomile. She's so close I can see the blond hairs sprouting along her top lip, see the capillaries in the whites of her eyes that are normally unseen. We're close enough to kiss. In truth I don't think I've been this close to a woman without kissing her or trying to kiss her. She moves even closer, only a fraction of the distance that's between us but it's significant, like as if someone's suddenly placed an ice-cold hand on my stomach.

Do you remember what happened?

I drank too much ... I must have fallen on the way home.

Pat was out with the telescope. He heard shouting on the strand. He went to take a closer look and saw you lying on the rocks.

That was really stupid of me.

You must have hit your head. When you're rested we'll drive to the surgery and the doctor can look at it.

I try to explain that it's nothing but she catches me by surprise, touching my hand, holding it, squeezing it before she lets go. Whatever I wanted to say about the bruise on my head has completely left my thoughts. She smiles and the lines the smile creates at the corners of her lips are unspeakably beautiful. I can't remember noticing that before on a woman, the follow-on effects of a smile, ripples on the serenest pond. She's wearing a fleece-jacket zipped to the throat, the normal kind of functional jacket the women around here wear. I try not to imagine what she's wearing underneath, or think about the fact that we're alone together in an isolated cottage. She's another man's wife. She doesn't belong to me but yet I'm still hoping she leans across again but this time loses her balance, falling across my face chest-first. The separation from Corinne must be getting to me. I force my mind to think about anything but Jemma Finch and how close she is, the warmth of her breath. She stands up briskly, looking and sounding more like her everyday self.

I've tidied up a bit and taken your clothes for laundering.

Don't go to any trouble.

There's no trouble to it. I'll drop them back when they're done.

I'm conscious I can bearly move due to the effects of hangover. I'm willing her to fluff the pillow again, to fuss over the bed-covers as she did earlier, her movements matronly, economical. She's not the woman I first met, harassed by the duties of motherhood, at the mercy of time. The vision of her jogging and the applications of care at my bed-side have turned that first impression inside out. I see now the wisdom of Pat Finch in her every atom. He'd have looked beyond the strictly physical when he first fell in love with her, seeing all the beauty he needed without having to probe for it. He'd have gone down on one knee to claim her, to offer her his world. I'm humiliated before her, both of us acting out the timeless roles of nurse and patient. I'm at her total mercy.

I've been a complete idiot.

You're on your own here John. That can't be easy.

I don't normally drink like that. It's not my style.

It happens ... You need to get some rest.

She smiles once more before leaving, turning quietly for the door. She closes it lightly behind her, taking time so that the mechanism slips shut noiselessly. She takes the same consideration at the front door, leaving without a sound. She'd have padded out of her little girl's room like that, on the night of the high temperature and all the other nights when they needed her.

She leaves behind a palpable tenderness in the bedroom, a kindness I haven't asked for and didn't expect. Her lovingness can't keep the next stream of thought at bay for long; the images of stupidity from the night before. I try but remember little about the second public bar or the third or the fourth or however it went. I shiver in pain, cringe beneath the duvet at the thought of how close I'd collapsed to the sea. It need have taken very little for the merciless tides to have claimed me, buried me forever in a wave of icy death. If Pat Finch hadn't heard the shouting and cursing before I fell there'd be nothing now only the eternal void. For what it's worth, Pat Finch saved my life, or his fascination with the cosmos save my life.

It's an agony to admit but I've never known such attentiveness before, not the same care that Jemma Finch has just shown me. It's a thought that burns almost as much as any other I've experienced by the sea, the thought that Corinne's applications of tenderness are dwarfed by another woman whom I hardly know. Love is so ideal when there's nothing to compare it against. Sleep comes as a brutal necessity, a complete submission to the torment of exhaustion and hangover.

The next sound I hear is another gull screaming by the bedroom window. And only seconds later, as my awakening mind is processing the sound of the coast beyond the bedroom window, I hear Pat Finch's voice. He's in the hallway, talking lightly on his phone. He's trying to keep his voice down but the intimacy of the lighthouse-cottage doesn't allow much to pass unheard. Wrapping a quilt around my shoulders I rush to the bathroom to vomit up the contents of a riotous stomach.

Finch has laid my laundered clothes neatly by the side of the bed, socks and towels laundered too. I'm fit enough to shower and shave, conscious of the time I'm spending in the bathroom as I know Pat Finch is waiting in the back-room of the cottage, by the window overlooking the sea. If he looks at the clippings on the table he'd see the quote from the killer Leconte, but would hardly understand the relevance of words so abstract. I'm ashamed of how he's seen me the night before – ashamed of so much.

Dressed and showered I appear before Finch in the back-room, apologising over and over in my mind before the words are actually verbalised in apology. It's another low moment in my life, standing in front of a man I like and admire after the events of the night before. He's quick to speak, the second I walk into the room.

They've spotted another hump-back whale off Raven Head. Different markings to the other one.

Pat ... I'm really sorry about last night.

Nothing to worry about. Happens all the time around here.

You saved my life.

One of his hands is up, waving it off as routine. He doesn't want to talk about it, as if there's nothing more natural than carrying a neighbour back to his bed after a night's drinking gone seriously wrong, like as if I've passed an unwritten test of coastal manliness. He's smiling shyly towards me, accepting the fragility that took me to the village pubs in the first place.

I've put you and your wife to a lot of trouble.

What makes you think that?

I don't know what to say, how to answer him. I wonder if she mentioned how I was staring at her as she jogged, or staring at a particular part of her anatomy to be exact. It's the isolation, the absence of Corinne. I feel the full vulnerability of the situation, my lack of status on the peninsula. I'm depending on Pat and Jemma Finch for so much, my survival to begin with. My sanity too. He pushes the fingers of one hand through the shock of his hair, grinning as if about to tell the joke of the year. He's scruffier than usual, what looks like oil spilt down the front of his jeans and jumper. He doesn't have to be here, doesn't have to give up any more of his time to help me out. Unless he too has troubles from the past to atone for. A deed done when nobody was looking or an act of mercy left undone. We've not got around to talking about it, the possibility that guilt runs through both our days and nights. He doesn't want tea or coffee and I haven't the courage to mention alcohol after what happened last night. I suddenly remember the absence of the most important possession I've got.

I can't find my phone.

I don't think you'd a phone with you when I found you last night. You might have left it in one of the pubs.

Pat Finch is sorry but he has to go, is dropping one of his girls off at the pony club. He touches my shoulder as he leaves; a gesture that feels overly intimate in the circumstances.

Don't worry ... things will work out okay. You know where we are if you need anything.

He looks pleased with himself, unconcerned about the past or the future. I envy him his normality, much the same kind of normality I should be enjoying back in Greenford if the past hadn't decided to wreck my life when it did. I wish the right context develops so as I can tell him he's made the right decisions in life, that he's not missed very much by living way out here on the peninsula.

After about an hour musing in the lighthouse-cottage I'm ready again for the might of the sea. My stomach is only fit for a mouthful or two of tap water and aspirin. Out on the headland two locals have let their dogs off the leash. They're slow men, long used to the sea and in no hurry to leave it. One of them whistles after a beagle chasing a low-flying gull. The beagle runs into tasselweed as the gull bellies upwards with a screech. The other dog, a black mongrel with curious white splotches on his snout, doubles back towards the four-wheeled drive they're arrived in. One of the men tries to jog on the strand but gives up with a laugh after twenty yards or so. His companion is laughing too. They've lived on the peninsula for so long they've given up all worries of bulging necks and torsos. They probably wobble their guts at the counter of the village pubs, laughing things off.

Pat Finch couldn't find it easy to survive among them, his sensitivities so long conjoined with the cosmos. He'd have stopped pointing out the wonder of the stars to the villagers a long time before. A buffoon bending over the pub counter, laughing in hoots, eager to tell his pals what Pat Finch had just said about the stars.

One of the men has paused to urinate against a sign erected among reedbed and willow. It's a warning that the area is under special protection under the E.U Birds directive. The other man calls out to me. There's an expectation that I should waste time with them in useless conversation, imparting my business for that day. But I'm too concerned about my missing phone, lost in the darkness of the previous night's foolishness. There's a vague hope rising that I might find it among the shingle and rocks of the strand.

The beagle hares out of the tassleweed and makes straight for me, tongue lapping, paws congealed with black mud and silt. I'd embrace him lovingly if it wasn't for the trouble Jemma Finch took to launder my clothes. I'd embrace him with all the love of a man starved of love, offer my face for to be drenched by his dripping tongue. He eyes me joyfully, skips and hesitates. Seeing the reluctance in my face he races on by.

I'm a stranger to the sea and to the lighthouse, but feel less of a stranger than the two men who've arrived to run their dogs on the strand. These men, gross and ponderous manifestations of humanity, are intruders on this stretch of the peninsula. It wouldn't take much for this layer of civilisation stretched tight over my skin and psyche to snap. What is it about the sea that brings out these frightening instincts of territorialism? I hurry towards the rocks beyond the dunes, the shortcut home, hurry away from the men with their high-wheeled jeep and running dogs. They don't understand that they are intruding.

It's pointless searching for a missing phone out here. The tidal patterns alone are enough to disperse entire warehouses of phones without a trace. Despondently, head throbbing from hangover, I walk through the green algae and seaweed exposed by the low tides. On a shingle beach I hope by some miracle to spot the phone among the debris of the sea-shore. I inquire into seawater pools, probing with the toe of a boot into aquatic vegetation, peering into a leakage from a sluice. Corinne always says I'm overly self-reliant, obvious issues with trust. Usually I say I only trust her. That's what she really wants to hear, what she's angling to hear. When two people are truly in love they don't need others. I only ever needed to trust her. We were happy within the limits of our mind-games.

During that last week in London I scrubbed the bathroom on three consecutive evenings; scouring enamel, polishing the taps. Corinne didn't say a lot but I know what she was thinking, that it wasn't necessary, that the bathroom was spotless to begin with. At one point she interrupted me and we looked at each other for some moments. Neither of us said anything but we both knew something was happening in my mind, the onset of an energy or tension that wasn't there before. It hung in the air between us, unsaid. So much remained unsaid.

I re-interpret Corinne's silences from months before, trying to see into her thoughts. She'd ask so many questions, all natural within the confines of our love. Then she'd enclose her conclusion within the privacy of her mind. Here by the sea I'm more and more convinced she's hoarded up reservations all along. All those imperturbable silences must have entailed a meaning. Did she speculate that as I hadn't made the effort to be there for my mother or my father as they deteriorated towards death, that I wouldn't make the effort to be there for her either? Was that it, fresh doubts?

The sea is rumbling a rebuff, the screams of gulls more mocking than before. The Little Egret from further up the shore is gliding inland. I understand why the green rippling sea is suddenly so inhospitable. It can kill too, just as effectively as a London underground train; salt gagging at the throat, lungs flooding. It wouldn't take much for a body to be floated out in sea-swirls, bloated in rituals of undercurrent voyages. And then maybe caught up in a herring-net, poked at curiously by a fisherman's gaff, or a trawler-man cursing the lousy luck of such an unwanted catch.

It's not as easy as London. The modern city makes it too easy, toeing the yellow safety line painted underfoot, all those strangers standing there for moral support. A non-singing, non-dancing chorus line for the last seconds leading to the finale. And then no more guilt, no more life either. Maybe that's what stops people, the fear it may not end. That there might be something to what the priests and rabbis are saying, some other dimension of consciousness. Yes as ludicrous as it sounds it's always a possibility, a dreamlike or disembodied existence. Further accusations, answers demanded, conversations with people from the past.

In a moment of panic I turn from the sea, running and then falling on the shingles. Only Corinne can save me, like she's always saved me. I picture her face and imagine her voice calling my name softly – begging the

essence of her soul that lives within me to take all this
away.

Chapter 12

Nothing beyond the working hours in the basement of the Goudron studio made any sense. Meandering walks beneath high Flemish gables and wrought-iron Brabant balconies, pissing statues and puppet-theatres. Nothing mattered except seeing Sonia.

Once I asked the old man who sometimes mopped the hotel corridors how a man like the night porter had come to work nights at the Hotel Eugene Plasky. He was a very old man, clearly senile, who reminisced lovingly about Leopold the second and Belgian's colonial days. He lived nearby, wandering in and out of the hotel at all hours of the day and night. He said he hadn't any why the night porter had come to work for Marco but that before he was sure he'd seen him working at the Musee des Egouts by the Boulevard du Midi in Anderlecht – the Sewer Museum.

Mostly I skipped the tram and walked from the hotel to the Goudron studio each morning, taking short-cuts through Rue du Mont-Blanc and Rue de la Victoire. Closing my eyes here by the sea, concentrating with the full powers of mind, I can see them again, the back-lanes of Brussels and how they first appeared to an unformed man.

Karpov won the final game in Baguio City and on the very next day my father finally died. They'd rung the Goudron studio with the news and M.Goudron beckoned me into his private office. He was happy with my work, working his correct grey hair into shape with the palm of one hand. I knew what he thought about me without him having to say it. He explained that naturally I'd have permission to return to Ireland to attend the funeral. I thanked him, but said that wouldn't be necessary, that I preferred to work on. He looked at me for a second or two longer than necessary and then nodded solemnly. As far as he was concerned that was fine with the studio, I could work on as ever, instead of organising a flight to home Ireland. For M. Goudron it was always about the work.

That day was like any other. The foot journey home nothing other than an accumulation of tired steps through that part of the city, a progression towards a room of dead flies and unopened letters in a pile by the bed. I sat and thought about it for hours, but his death had no impact on me, none at all. I didn't care if the man lived or died. We were strangers to each other, thrown together in a construct by which children are fed and accommodated, and whereby class and status and other matters are demarcated. Only Sonia mattered. In the Hotel Eugene Plasky the foyer and corridors were emptier than before. Guests and visitors didn't come and go as freely like they used to. Bathrooms and hallways were uncleaned, mice and spiders finding their way into every crack of the masonry, the most elementary maintenance work left ignored. Marco hung around much like he always did, but looked disinterested and often distracted, like a man waiting for a train and thinking only of his destination. Nobody checked if the front doors were locked at night. Stray cats wandered in from the street, luminous eyes like feral midnight spirits in the corridors. The doors of empty rooms swung open, exposing the neglect within. One night a drunk roared in the hallways and kicked at several doors. He woke up the entire building looking for an old girlfriend who used to stay there. Marco's voice was heard, the drunk's voice rising argumentatively. Quickly the hotel lapsed into a sullen quietness again. In the morning a trail of blood splatter stained the floor-tiles from the foyer to the street.

The hotel was literally falling to pieces. Only one thing kept me there, only Sonia mattered. It'd have been easy enough to find somewhere else to stay as the city wasn't overcrowded. But I hung around, knowing that even if I hadn't seen Sonia on any given day that she wasn't far away. I'd speak to Marco in passing, our words limited. He didn't mention the disappearance of the night porter and the deterioration of the building. I didn't bother asking.

The post-death stain of blood discolouration on the same skin that sent men out of their minds with desire. Sonia going green, brain-cells dying in millions, her thought-processes ending, pancreas digesting itself. Only the whites of her eyes visible, muscle flaccidity at the moment of death, her limber corpse suggestive of the supernatural, the absence of rigor mortis. Intestinal bacteria bloating her with putrid gas. How can the human mind comprehend a woman as beautiful as Sonia tumbling down the path of all flesh? Tongue and eyes protruding, intestines beginning to push out through her vagina and anus. The beautiful Sonia. If the diamond-dealer willing to kill for her or the Gypsies with their knives could have seen her in death - what would they have thought? Her body swelling, cadavernine seep from the nose ... Sonia dead.

There wasn't anything anyone could have done about it. I'd become an empty vessel waiting to be filled by fate. There was nowhere to turn, no way of wriggling out of what fate held for me. Marco noticed it, maybe the only one who did. By then he was too preoccupied to talk about it. He hadn't time for much beyond sitting in the foyer drumming his fingernails on the reception-desk and waiting for visitors. Only once more did I see him meeting with the freak with the tattooed fingers. They spoke in raised voices in the cubicle behind the reception-desk. I didn't see tattooed-fingers again after that day. But even now, on certain nights, I feel his presence.

The day in question wasn't any different than any other day. Mussels were in season, sold cheaply with chips in the cafes of Barriere-St Gilles. I ate at a pavement table even though I'd little appetite. Eyes downwards on the way home, mind straddled between the various tasks set that week by M.Goudron. The front doors of the hotel were swinging open, a pane in one of the groundfloor windows facing the street broken; one shard jutting up like a dusty fang. A letter in the sign above the door was missing, the letter 'e' in the word 'Eugene'. There was nobody around, leaves and debris from the street blown by breezes into the foyer. Nothing happening, not in the few rooms yet occupied or in that room of dead flies at the end of the ground-floor corridor. The predictable stench from the back-yard bins permeated the lower floors. There was nothing to do except hang around the foyer waiting for Sonia to rush in or out of the building. After a few minutes of doing just that I went back to my room, lying in the squalid bed, looking indolently at the myriad patterns in the cracked ceiling.

It was too late by then. I can't see how helpful it may be to try and understand the role of others in the whole miserable business. It was too late for all that, the icons from a mother's loving hand discarded among the hotel's filth. In the mostly empty hotel nobody came or went, no doors banging at one in the morning or muffled dead-weights dragged through the corridors. Nobody moaned in the nearby rooms. Idly I wandered the landings and stairways, curious as to the terminal decline of the building, kicking at the accumulations of debris on the floors. It was so empty I almost missed the night porter. There was a calmness too, a prescience, a hunch that a moment's relief was on its way. The desires of an unformed man were heaping one on top of the other like amputated limbs in the operating theatre of a hospital in a besieged city.

Expectation intensified in the hotel's neglected corridors and stairways, a promise amid the filth that there'd be a dissipation of desire. An excitement too, to think that I might soon experience the world without Sonia's existence hammering at the minutes and seconds like a mania. How that might happen I didn't at that time know, but somewhat that's how it felt.

The first sighting of Marco that evening was out of the ordinary. I saw him from the hotel foyer, in a cream-coloured Mercedes parked out the front of the hotel. It was the kind of car people stop to notice. He climbed from the back-seats into the street, conversing with the two men in the front through an opened window. He looked relaxed, among friends. He shouted a parting word or two as the car pulled away. I'd a good view of him as he crossed the road and began climbing the steps towards the front door of the hotel. It wasn't like he'd caught me by surprise. Without any trouble I'd have easily slipped unseen into my room if I wanted to, spent what remained of the evening listening to the radio and staring trance-like at the cracked ceiling. And then escape – just take the papers I needed and go, never to return. But I didn't do that as a force rooted me to the floor-tiles of the foyer. I'd only come across that force once before, on that hill of rain and tram-lines.

The hotel was desolate. Marco was on the front steps with lips parted in the imitation of a grin, gold caps gleaming reflections of the dying evening sun. Yet there was time to escape, to get the hell out of there, to slipping from his influence. But I just stood there like a fool, waiting for him to arrive in the foyer.

John ... you looking for me?

No ... not particularly.

You're wondering where everyone is?

The hotel is quiet.

Things are changing.

He tried to put me at ease, smiling and touching me briefly on one arm. I could see he was preoccupied with his private thoughts, far more on his mind than his last few guests. He crossed the hotel foyer, stopping as an afterthought and turning around, a revelation breaking on his crude features. I dallied by the front door of the building, not knowing how to shape the evening, drowning in inertia and inadequacy. He tried to smile but couldn't quite manage it, the direction of his thoughts leaning hard on his options for expression.

When you finish up in Brussels, he said. Where will you go?

I haven't really thought about it.

Nothing good happens for you here.

No … nothing.

I have one idea ... come with me.

A sheen-like melting asphalt gleamed from his black trousers – a kind of leather or pvc material. An ear-ring glittered from the lobe of one ear, a cheap and silvery fake. I knew about jewellery even at a glance. He looked foolish and contrived. That style didn't suit him. He moved differently too, as if he'd sprained a tender muscle and didn't want to risk a further strain. I'd have asked him why he'd dressed like that, why he'd taken the trouble to smooth back his mane with hair-balm, but I didn't trust myself not to sound impertinent.

Placing a hand lightly on my shoulder, he led me across the foyer and into the ground-floor corridor that connected to the stairways. He'd have performed that routine often before, the charming patterns of a shark. He measured his words and gestures, as exact as a salesman. Something was about to happen. It just had to happen and it had to be big. I felt it'd be pointless to resist. It had all been leading to those very moments. Instead of turning and running for the door I allowed the seduction of Marco's words to lead me towards the stairs and then upwards.

Nothing stirred and there wasn't a sound from anywhere in the building or from the street outside. Blood from the late-night drunk that Marco had thrown out had dried into a dark brown and ominous splash on the floor of the foyer. Nobody had made an effort to wipe it up. There even wasn't the sound of a stray cat, the creak of a floorboard. The silence wasn't natural, but maybe that's just how I'm remembering it. Maybe there was noise, but if there was I didn't hear it.

I've blocked out the details of that actual time so effectively from my thoughts that I'm sweating cold just thinking about them now. But there mustn't be any hesitation, not when the alternative is considered. It's why I've come here after all, to isolate that moment and in doing so hope to find a perspective to hold onto. There's no other reason to be here in the lighthouse-cottage, separated from Corinne, living through it all again.

Together we ascended the stairs towards the attic-rooms, Marco guiding me on like a sightless innocent, a hand lightly on my shoulder. I paused on the first step that led to the attic-rooms. He'd have seen the uncertainty, the look on my face. He took his hand away from my shoulder, gesturing with his other hand for me to continue on up.

I want to give you a gift.

What kind of gift?

A gift nobody else can give you.

The stairs leading to his lair were too tight for us to walk side by side so I went on ahead. The attic-rooms were mostly in darkness, light spilling from only one room into the corridor. From where we stood we heard the groaning straightaway, the faint groaning of a female. He pointed with one finger in the direction of the opened door, eyebrows raising very briefly and then winking. It was as if we were set to play a joke on someone. There was something seriously wrong with him – anyone could see that in the tight hallway of the attic-rooms of the hotel. Nobody reasonably satisfied within the ordinary bounds of normality would have gone within a mile of him. But by then it was too late, light dying outside in the street and throughout the city. Softly we approached the opened door until we stood outside it looking in. Sonia was lying on the same bed where I'd seen her before, limp as if drugged, quietly groaning.

He gestured me into the bedroom ahead of him, not pushing but almost pushing. Studded leather belts and straps of varying sizes littered the floor. She'd picked up a coin-sized bruise on one side of her forehead, red marks on her wrists. She wore a long white nightdress, sweat breaking on her arms and forehead. She groaned and moved her head to one side. Marco stepped towards her, touching her lovingly on the side of the face, smoothing back a strand of hair falling across her eyes.

She's mine, he said. I own her just like you can own a beautiful piece of jewellery. Do you understand?

I don't think I understand.

She must do everything I tell her. But she didn't do so ... that's why I'm angry.

He said he was angry but he didn't look or sound angry; just more detached than usual. The pupils of his eyes were dilated, like nails hammered into a yellowing membrane, ludicrous in black clothes, dressed up stupidly in somewhere like the Hotel Eugene Plasky.

My first thought was that he'd poisoned her, as the room smelt lightly of chemicals. From the drawer of a bureau pushed against one wall Marco retrieved a leather device not unlike a bridle. He held it up momentarily like a prize, grinning malevolently. He returned to the bedside and I could see he was holding a kind of choker made from leather with a three foot lead dangling from it. In seconds he had it looped around Sonia's bare neck, with the deftest of hands as if he'd done it lots of times before. He played the lead through his fingers until it was taut. Sonia was oblivious to this new game, groaning and turning her head from side to side. Marco looked directly at me, holding the lead loosely in one hand.

If one of us pulled hard on this lead for two minutes ... then Sonia is gone forever.

Why would we do that?

You don't want to know that.

Are you going to pull on that thing?

No ... you will pull on it.

Just at that point here was nothing to buffer Marco's instructions, nothing or no one to offer a saner angle. Helpless before him, stripped down psychologically to curiosity and base desires. Excited to be so close to Sonia, to have more than the usual few seconds of visual contact as she hurried in and out of the hotel. Marco held the lead up close to my face. "I know you love her. But all your life you cannot have a woman like her. Men dream of her ... but they cannot have her."

Is she drugged?

Yes ... she is drugged.

Is she in pain?

That is not important. But I want you to listen closely, because what I'm going to say now is important.

Circumstances or necessity or other inexplicable reasons had created that scenario, where only the practical mattered. Other concepts like right or wrong didn't exist in the attic-rooms of the hotel, the sanctity of life and all the righteous concepts constructed in the mind of the civilised man. I was only conscious of Marco's voice and Sonia of course, lying there so helplessly.

You can have her for one hour. What you do with her is your business. But then you must pull on this until she stops breathing.

He looked at me even, turning the angle of his head and narrowing his eyes as if trying to see inside me. I was staring at Sonia, afraid to take my eyes off her for a second. I must have thought about the hours I'd sacrificed, hanging around the hotel foyer and corridors in the hope of seeing her even for a second or two. There was nothing more important than waiting to see Sonia. The other events in my life at the time meant nothing, the working days at the Goudron studio, my dying father, that chess match in the Philippines. Only Sonia mattered. I'd have waited for hours and hours if I knew she was going to pass through the hotel foyer. I don't know what that made me, or what name easily tags onto people who behave like that. But that's how it was. And there she was, lying so close by that if I held out my hand it'd brush against her hair. Marco held out one end of the choke-lead he was holding. I took a step back from him. I don't get it I said. Why does this have to happen to her?

If you accept the offer of one hour alone with her, then you must do it. If you don't like the offer ... then go back to your room.

I couldn't form words into any kind of verbal response, at least not straightaway. I don't know how many seconds, or how many utterly blank thoughts it took to speak. In that time Marco said nothing, waiting patiently with the choke-lead in his hand as if the phenomenon of time was of no significance. I ran my eyes along Sonia's neck and shoulders, the tiny pearls of sweat along the hairline of her forehead.

When I said the word 'yes' my eyes never deviated from her, afraid that if I looked away it'd break the spell, that somehow she'd disappear and that I'd never see her again. Marco heard what I'd said the first time, but he wanted me to say it again, wanted to make sure I'd go through with it.

Yes okay, I said. I'll do it.

I didn't turn from her to judge the effect my words had on Marco. He said nothing further, just handed me one end of the choke-lead and silently left the room. He closed the door with softly and then I heard the locking-mechanism slotting home.

At the end of the allocated hour I held the lead of the leather choker in one hand for several seconds, not thinking about anything in particular, not experiencing any dominant emotion. Then I pulled on the lead with all my strength, turning away as her face changed colour. I thought I heard a click, the hyoid bone snapping. But I can't be sure. It may just have been a spring moving in the bed under the strain. Blood-vessels in her brain congesting, an asphyxiation at a dead hour. She died as ingloriously as a dog choking on its vomit; pin-prick haemorrhages bursting on her chest and breasts, her death dispassionate in the absence of fingernail marks on my skin, the absence of contusions from the final struggles.

I loosened the choke-lead and her head slewed to one side, showing the leather circumscription of the collar on her neck. Covered in sweat, shaking from head to foot, I'd lost track of time. I couldn't tell if I'd been alone with her for minutes or hours. Then the door clicked open and I knew it was all over, that everything had ended, that nothing could ever be the same. Marco was standing there, looking satisfied with the result. He pushed her head roughly where she lay lifeless on the bed, nodding and grinning in approval, pleased the deal was complete.

Chapter 13

Vegetation floating on a stream inland is startling in diversity. I follow a reed swamp on the other side of the dunes, past bog and heathland, into alluvial wet woodlands. The stream is a surprise, yellowish water-lily and what might be duckweed on its surface. A frog is exposed between the stream-edge and rough gorse, vulnerable to predators or the gleeful hands of a passing boy.

I follow the run of the stream past a copse of oaks flanked by bracken and brambles, intoxicated by the wildness. A lapwing takes flight from a willow tree and tufted ducks are flying out to sea. The stream meanders beneath a fence that demarcates a rectangle of arable land from the coastal wilderness; an intrusion of farming business into a land that conjures mythical concepts. It's easy to lose oneself in this nature, to forget all human concerns and follies. This is the same land Pat Finch knew growing up, that helped form him. It's left its influence on him, a perspective of other-worldliness. Deep into the greenery the reality is as alien to ordinary days as night-skies through a telescope.

The serenity of the streamside is semi-surreal, a retreat for dreamers. But kamikaze midges fly madly for the sensitive spots on the eye. It's a relief to leave them behind, to return to the comfort of the sea. I re-trace my steps along the stream to the coastal trail and beyond to the irrepressible lighthouse. By the sea, only after minutes, heads are breaking the water. Otters or seals – from this distance it's impossible to tell which. The sky is uncertain, a weak shade of grey without substance. The wintering waterbirds are riotous overhead, gulls swooping. The physical presence of the sea is overpowering, thoughts of leaving it creating a personal hurt like when a beloved possession is threatened. I make a preliminary estimate of what it would take to stay here forever; to sleep and wake with the sea lapping against my dreams. Patient and avuncular, paternal like the cosmos, watching the Finch girls grow into young women; conversing with Jemma and Pat Finch. Contrite until death, watching for opportunities to anonymously re-pay for what was taken in the past. And then withered foetal-like at the end of life to beg Jemma Finch to suckle me on her mothering paps; fossilize among the detritus of the waves and tides, hands held out to fate, dying with the taste of her milk on my lips.

In practical terms it'd be routine, a mere matter of an hour on Pat Finch's computer and several phone-calls to London. After a private word with the auctioneer there'd be the usual forms to sign. I'd be free to live out what days remain here by the sea. I think of Corinne, the ache that comes with the feeling that I'm losing her, or that I've never deserved her in the first place. That impression is a painful stranglehold the longer I'm here by the sea, the more I search the past for answers, that I never deserved her in the first place.

A dog barks hoarse from its throat, forcing the reality of the coast back into focus. It's an uplifting bark, more like a laugh than anything else. I turn around to see a golden Labrador running towards me, shaggier and fatter than dogs of that breed tend to be. The eyes are shining with love and trust, tongue hanging loosely down one side of an opened mouth, skipping playfully with the run. Pat Finch is grinning and waving one hand in the distance, sharing in the joy the Labrador is brings to the coast. It's one of those dogs whose simple presence among humans raises smiles. I play with his ears and rub his neck. The touch of his tongue on my hand and the dog breath are an thrilling connection to childhood. When she jumps up on me she completes a loop to the childhood dogs we played with in our dreary little town. And an essence too beyond childhood and adolescence.

Pat Finch is laughing, head tilting back, the playfulness of the animal lifting him to a higher mood. She's a mature bitch, dried-up teats, stomach hanging in folds. She might be a rescue, the owner keeling into the rhododendrons and dying contrary to all expectations. I think about our cats in Greenford and how they were alive to our every movement, how they settle down to sleep when we settle down, wake for the day when we wake. Pat Finch is quickly beside me, stroking the bitch's head, sharing in the joy. She belongs to Jemma's sister, he says. She loves the sea.

Dogs like her are gifted with healing so I bend, allowing her tongue to explore my forehead. Then I press my head against the fur of her neck, ruffling her ears, touching my nose on her cold snout. If only I'd have known a creature like her during that year in Brussels nothing sinister or ugly could have happened. I'd have taken her for endless walks through the city. She'd have saved me from the nights that destroyed me. Finch is laughing with joy, then a second later he's solemn, face lengthening as he pats the animal's rump.

She had the cancer a few years back, he says. Touch and go.

The dog?

No the sister. Jemma is very close to her. I take the dog now and then to give them a break.

You'd hate somewhere like London Pat ...

People get used to things. You got used to it.

The bitch is jumping up on Finch, imprinting muddy paws on his sports' top. He's hugging her playfully, loving her as much as he loves his own intimate circle. We're constructed from the same forces, predictable products of childhoods shaped by church-raffles and flag-days, Corpus Christi processions and nine-Friday penances. That much is obvious as we enjoy the animal's presence. We find a personal history in each other naturally, knowing that very little divides the dark midland town I was brought up in from the damp fields of Finch's childhood. At moments in our conversations it's like we're trying to fathom out the precise event that determined our adult lives.

He chases after the Labrador with a laugh, swooping on a stick of driftwood on the shingles as if it's the find of the day. He hoists it in an overhead throw as far as he can along the strand. The dog is barking as she goes after the stick, teats swinging. Finch jogs the short distance between us, happier than I've yet seen him. We fall into an easy step together, in the direction chosen by the dog.

Did you notice anything last night?

Like what?

That's what my father always did, answer a question with another question. He was a master at it. There was

166

hardly a situation he didn't fire back a question that stumped the second party. Occasionally he was witty, but mostly defensive or sarcastic. The sneer came to him naturally, especially when it came to his own off-spring. It's odd how he returns to my thoughts here by the sea, more than how he did for years. All the freedom and emotional distance mean little when his voice returns to my inner-ear, as if his complete indifference to our lives went on yesterday or the week before. There's more than a hint there'll never be an escape from it - the damage done.

Finch grins foolishly, then gurns momentarily. It's not a simple matter to read his expression, to work out if there's a joke coming or another warning about the sea or the weather. It's a trait I've noticed in the local pubs, a disconnection between expression and word. It's impossible to tell if they're about to laugh at a joke they heard earlier or announce their own permanent destruction.

I mean did you not find it very quiet?

I didn't notice.

That's surprising.

Did something happen?

He pulls the same pathetic little conversational stunt that he's pulled before, drawing me in, poking alive a spark of curiosity and then going all silent. It's not quite infuriating, but one can predict not so distant circumstances where it might be. He must drive Jemma Finch nuts at times. I don't know if he's noticed a wince of irritation, how I look away but he doesn't draw it out unnecessarily. Continues mischievously without the prompt he's fishing for.

The foghorn on the lighthouse ... they've switched it off.

Why would they do that?

They're switching all the horns off. You see boats these days navigate by technology, satellites and what have you.

I didn't notice.

But if a boat's equipment breaks down then at least the fog-horn will keep her off the rocks.

That's a pity.

That's how it's going. Soon they'll shut down the lighthouse itself.

We pause on the headland, contemplating a world without lighthouses.

They'd replace them with a gadget at the very top of a mast, signals directed by satellite out to sea; the gadget unseen among a contortion of other electronic devices. What kind of world would that be, without lighthouses? Finch is sadly shaking his head from side to side. I thought you'd have noticed ... a man who appreciates life on the peninsula.

Sorry ... I didn't notice.

The bitch has turned back, her tail down, abandoning the mission to retrieve the stick Finch expended so much energy in throwing, distracted by gulls and sea-scents. That annoys him, but he pretends it's nothing, that he hasn't registered the breach of loyalty in the ancient bonds of man and dog. Her eyes are softer, an almost indiscernible whine in her throat. She's a sensitive being. One could easily imagine her understanding our conversation, or at least understanding the conversation's dominant emotion – an emotion of loss. She whines more discernibly, as if she too sees it, the changes in the world. Finch watches her intently; then looks out to sea, sighing as if longing to be involved for once in a great global adventure. He says he wants to skirt the lighthouse with the bitch, tire her out before taking her back to her ailing owner. I don't want to hold him up, look critically upwards as if predicting rain. The bitch lunges with a snap of her jaws, running at gulls, frightening them into emergency take-offs. She's enjoying the sea, the hours of careless release from a house of cancer. Pat Finch is worried about the bump on my head, wants to drop me off at the medical surgery in the town.

Someone should take a look at it.

It's nothing. My own fault anyhow.

You should get it checked out.

It's just a bump. I've had worse falling out of bed.

He shrugs one shoulder in a curious gesture, pulls a childish face. What does it mean to him anyhow? Men fall on the rocks on the way home from foolish outings, or lose their wits in drink, raging against the moon and tides. I'm hardly the first to stumble on the peninsula in a hapless tirade against fate. He looks at me cautiously, before settling his gaze out to sea.

I've had an idea. You can keep the dog this weekend. Jemma's sister and her family are away until Tuesday.

Why would I do that?

She's great company. A man wouldn't be lonely with her around.

Who said I'm lonely?

That caught him off guard, sounding jarringly implausible for the circumstances. The responding look on his face says it all. After all the ground we've covered, all the progress towards trust, it's inexcusable. To say that to his face, who said I'm lonely? The passing gulls can see the loneliness scarred eternally into my every expression. Why would I think Pat Finch can't? He's offended, our friendship taking a backward step or two. He walks on abruptly, speaking over one shoulder.

It's only an idea. It's quiet out here at night.

It's nice of you to offer.

Mistruth is more naked here by the sea, more easily illuminated. In an impersonal city of strangers even the unsophisticated can become masters of subterfuge if they stick with it. But not here, not with the lighthouse and all it stands for looking on. On this stretch of the peninsula every single human expression is an occurrence, an occasion for common analysis. He'll think less of me because of that lapse in honesty. How easily the words fell from my lips, as if I've learnt nothing from the past.

There's a gap opening up between us as we walk the strand, a mood that even the joyful presence of the bitch can't dissipate. I'm angry at why I'm here, without Corinne's love and influence. That face on the London underground could have only belonged to one man. This perverse loop in time in all his doing, this questing for another perspective on an old occurrence. Dissonance and the anxiety increasing, a residual ache. That crime buried again and again in my psyche, returning like it all happened the day before yesterday. In the hours before leaving London no other thought or feeling was strong enough to slip pass and dominate the memories from the Hotel Eugene Plasky.

There'd been late-night phonecalls to a helpline that didn't help. Only after minutes the helpline volunteer was frustrated by the responses to his questions. He'd most likely had a bellyful before I'd even called. Not that it could have helped anyhow, because I couldn't say what I needed to say. Since seeing that face on the train there's a process going on that I'm almost helpless to influence. It's a mental state Pat Finch recognises. He sees it clearly as if it's pressing down on him too. He sees the evidence of where this is going written all over me. It spooks him more than it ought to.

He wants to say something about my loneliness or my stated lack of loneliness, to contextualise the tensions between us. But the bitch is running wild, straying into the mudflats. It'd only take a minute in the black ooze and even a weekend of hot scrubs wouldn't clean her off. Finch steps back a yard or two, jamming two fingers and a thumb between his lips. If he hadn't stepped away the whistle would have caught me painfully in one ear. We watch her with interest as she hesitates with her tail in the air, sniffs at the route ahead, the fun she'd have chasing gulls through the mudflats. A second whistle has her turning. He looks at me critically, as if not yet over the disappointment about what I said about not being lonely.

I've elevated the telescope-mount. You should come over this evening and try it out. Say at about nine.

Why not?

You'll like it. The stars take a man's mind off things.

I've time to quickly stroke the bitch's head in parting, then they're off in the direction of the lighthouse, feeding off each other's enthusiasm for the shore. They're similar in many ways, so similar that if they shared the same species they'd be doppelgangers. The bitch exceeds herself, running harder than an animal her age and breed is expected to run, teats flapping madly from side to side. She's excited by the sea and the gulls, running off tensions from the house of illness.

There was no mistaking that face on the Central line; a face decades older than when I first knew it. The hair worn longer, greying without any intervention of dye. People didn't give him a second glance as he sat there so self-composed in the crowded carriage. If a Londoner did happen to look at him for a reason of his or her own they'd have marked him down as a foreigner, almost certainly a continental. In two seconds they'd have logged him mentally as a tourist and then have forgotten about him forever. But I recognised him instantly as Marco from the Hotel Eugene Plasky.

He didn't look as cruel or as dangerous as when I knew him first. The years had changed him, taken away his energy so that he looked harmless, almost inanimate. If anyone had to pass judgement on him there and then on the underground they'd probably guess he was a retired hotel chef or postal worker, placid and compliant, with photographs of grandchildren in his wallet. Events in life had altered him, whatever he'd gone through. But it was definitely Marco sitting there alone, travelling quietly on a London underground train.

From where I stood by the door of the cramped train I looked away, caught up in a rising panic, a state of near-breathlessness. Fearfully, I sneaked further glances his direction. He sat self-absorbed and content, a newspaper folded on his knee, no signs of torment anywhere on his face. My mind struggled to process it, to work out what it meant. It was just another working day, just another commute to another meeting with Peter Branwitz. And there in the middle of that ordinary day Marco from that hotel of horrors sat placidly, looking like he was on his way to the West End to buy a birthday gift for a family member. There were at least a dozen stops before Ealing Broadway and then a bus home to Greenford, but I got off at the next stop. I glanced one final time before stepping onto a frantic platform of rapidly-moving forms. He sat there as if lost in contemplation, unperturbed. He didn't notice me, or if he did it didn't show anywhere on his face. He didn't seem to notice anyone, oblivious to the harassed metropolitan commuters running late for appointments and tourists with intrusive cameras. I slumped onto the nearest platform bench, weak in the legs, conscious of an anxiety that I'd no idea would soon drive me out of London and to the sanctuary of the sea.

After Brussels I feared he'd come looking for me, but he never did. He allowed me to walk out of the Hotel Eugene Plasky, to walk away from Brussels without any comment on what had happened. He'd have found me without much trouble in Brussels or Dublin. In the vastness and impersonality of London he'd have found it harder, but he'd have found me there if he really tried. In the loneliest corner of the planet he'd have found me, if he'd put his mind to it. But he didn't come looking for me, satisfied with the deal we'd struck, with how I followed the instructions. When I met Corinne we fell in love straightaway, new directions in life opening up. The events in Brussels faded until it was hard to actually believe they happened. Corinne changed me, London changed me, so that I grew beyond that unformed mind that fate had used so conveniently for its own design. One day I must have just stopped worrying about it, the memories fading to almost nothing.

Up until that ordinary working day the past held no power, was nothing more than a minor irritant. Now and then Corinne joked about how I stand daydreaming in the back garden, just staring out at nothing instead of carrying on with the weeding. It wasn't important, didn't matter. Nothing mattered other than our lives together in Greenford. Everything other than our love was tangential. You could say that life was perfect, or perfect as can be, before I seen an older Marco on that crowded train.

About halfway along the coastal trail to the village a light rain begins falling, warm on the skin, therapeutic. Jerking up the hood of the duffel I proceed monk-like, mentally constructing and then de-constructing the quickest routes back to Greenford. There's nobody on foot, only eternal cars passing in both directions on the coast road, long rigs heading for the Rosslare ferry. Closer to the village the gate to the church is unlocked; a hesitant invitation. The grey pebble-dash on the angular building and the greyness of the skies conjoin in a picture of total misery, a symbol of a distinctly Irish sufferance. It's ominous and fearful, a killing ground for the human spirit. It could be the childhood church from our dreary midland town with its predictions of doom and death, ridiculous men in costume repeating cant. At each gathering they slaughtered the spirit of the young with hollow words and vague references to blood. Now the churches are almost empty, gates mostly locked, rain falling.

When there is an alternative people grasp it, an escape from the fear and guilt, from the creed of withered old men on downbeat Sundays. How dispassionately I pushed my mother's icons and beads into the rubbish-pails of the Hotel Eugene Plasky. Seeing Marco on that otherwise banal journey re-injected fear and guilt back into my bloodstream. At first I ran it through the usual thought processes, searching for a blueprint from which to work from, a way of reading it with clarity. I thought it might have a link to the guilt of not showing up for my father's death-bed, my poor input into the care of my mother in her years of madness. People talk about Catholic guilt, the potency of the Irish variety, but I'd pushed all that aside for the sake of a near-perfect life with Corinne. And then after so long, out of nowhere, a

torrent of guilt, an urge to lean into the path of a
Central line train.

In the hours and days after seeing Marco on that train it
came into startling focus, livid and persecutory in the
mind's eye, refusing to budge. It manifested in my
consciousness as a simple question asked over and
over, 'why did you do it?' When I analysed it nothing
made sense. Why should I have harmed a person like
Sonia, done the things I done to her? She'd done me no
harm. Her existence may have tormented me but she'd
done me no deliberate harm. I ran it through my mind
in bed at night with Corinne, as she studied her papers
or read the work of her pupils. Courtroom humiliations,
strangers who'd never actually seen Sonia or the effect
she had on men handing down condemnations, cell-
doors banging and institutionalised food. Corinne
shamed too, her life in Greenford ruined. 'John how
could you have done such a thing?' That's the only
words she'd have said to me after she'd taken it all in,
realised what a monster she'd been living with. Rather
than all that I'd have jumped in front of a train.

A priest walks briskly into view from the side of the
church, holding a book or prayer missal above his head
against the rain. But the rain has ended. His face is
young and smooth, his walk graceful. He's preoccupied
with the duties of the day, in a hurry to get things done.
He sees me and stops, focusing on where I stand,
leaning forward slightly in a gesture of curiosity.
Quickly I walk on, disgusted at myself for gawping at
churches, interrupting jittery clergymen. As I enter the
village one thought stands ahead of all others, that this
must be the ultimate destination one the road leading
from the altar and the convoluted suffering of those
deadbeat Sundays. It's a destination of solitude where

one forever tries to work out the answers to fundamentally impossible questions. It often feels close to certain types of madness, these neurotic conditions of the modern world. Sometimes, especially at night, it feels almost close to freedom.

In the quietest village pub a foreigner is serving the bar, an outsider just like me. She's pretty but severe, burdened beyond her years, lips pursing. She looks at me as if I'm a hobo or a drunk just about to negotiate for the first drink of the day on credit. She's without a manager or colleague to reassure her, to give her the okay. I take off my duffel, shake rain from it before draping it on a chair near a storage-heater. She doesn't approve of how I'm making myself at home, frowning, eyes narrowing as she rubs a cloth over an already clean portion of the counter-top. Without thinking I almost order whisky but then pause. Reflecting for a moment on the recent whisky adventure I order a club sandwich and a bottle of stout. She's unfriendly, naturally cold, but when she turns around the tightness of her jeans redeems all. She'd easily fill the vacuum of a younger man's obsession, just like that earlier time when Sonia filled the vacuum of a deadly obsession.

I'm miserable without a phone-link to Corinne, like I've lost a limb not just a phone. On the high stool at the deserted counter I spend the next twenty minutes or so mostly silent. The bar-worker is wary, harbouring the usual preconceptions if her expressions are anything to go on – more nervous than necessary. I repeat a harmless joke about the weather I heard in a pub a few days back but she doesn't understand. I re-phrase it in baby words but she still doesn't get it. I tell her to forget about it, that it's not important.

She's about the same age as that unformed man who used my name and appeared in my body all those years ago in Brussels. I try to remember what it must be like for her, in a country she's not used to, her English faltering. She'd make mistakes, trapped in language. Does she look at me and think I was born like this? Could she possibly conceive that I too was once young? I try not to look at her so that she'd notice, curious for clues as to how she sees the world. She's busy wiping down the counter-top, using far more vigour than what's necessary.

Our relationship to each other symbolises an important essence, but I'm not sure what exactly. We're strangers on either side of a counter. During the same span of moments there are innumerable scenarios all around the world, strangers who'd stumbled into roles among other strangers for a multitude of mostly practical reasons. That strand of thinking leads me quickly to an abyss of fear. If I lost Corinne that's exactly how it'd be, the company of strangers until whenever it ends. When I leave the counter the bar-maid is visibly relieved. I'm relieved too, hopeful I'll never see her again.

The village post-office is too crowded on the first visit, so I turn back, walk the length of the village, skirt the trees at the roundabout. On the second sortie it's tolerable. In the telephone booth I dial the familiar number, the only number I know by heart. In the dialling tone I can hear the phone ringing in Greenford. Physically I can hear it ringing even though I know that's impossible. I can hear it ringing way down in that part of me that's yearning for home. I visualise the cats lazing in their favourite roosts in the hallway and living-room. The spare room that we converted into a workshop, my library of design-manuals stacked alphabetically on pine-shelves fixed along one wall. That old washing-machine that came from who knows where rotting at the bottom of our garden. I promised Corinne a hundred times or more than I'd get rid of it but somehow it was always easier to allow it to rust in the high grass. As the phone in Greenford rings I picture Corinne's old Volkswagen with the timber frame-struts parked in our driveway, my eyes closed, ear pressed hard to the earpiece on the phone. I listen as intently as I've ever listened, waiting for Corinne's voice. There's no answer. I hang up and dial out the number for the second time, but again there's no answer.

I hang up and leave swiftly, ignoring how a few locals at the clerk's counter are looking towards me expectantly. I don't know if it's because I've banged the phone unnecessarily hard into its cradle or if its just the orthodoxy of the peninsula requiring me to join in the banality of their conversation. That's what they'd appreciate, to stand idly disclosing my business for the day, laughing at dry jokes at someone else's expense. There'd be a dispensation in return, a nod or two of approval. But instead of another phoney performance in words I acknowledge them with the briefest facial manipulation and leave immediately.

Outside the skies have lightened, a blue opening of optimism on the sea's horizon. But the winds are bitter, ravaging the coast like ice-fingers jabbing blindly. On the entire walk back to the sanctuary of the cottage I'm imagining the scenarios Corinne is probably occupied with back home. Passing Finch's bungalow and in the final paces to the lighthouse-cottage the sea-winds are even sharper. I doze off undressed on the divan, grateful for a door to close out on the world. In sleep I imagine sea-monsters with foot-wide fangs at high-tide, breaching the promontory. They surround the lighthouse-cottage in a conspiracy, hoping for a wrong move. I wake from the nightmare, shouting and falling from the divan to the floor. I'm disorientated as the terror passes, day descending into evening. Without Corinne's presence the prevailing reality is unbearable. There's nothing evident but the urgings of conscience. The hellishness is rescued by Pat Finch's offer, the promise of the views through the telescope disproportionate to what they are or could ever be.

There's two hours to go to the time he mentioned. The passing of time in cities like London is savaged by necessity. It's a simple luxury to discard calendars here by the sea, clocks and special phones that beep out prompts for impending appointments. If someone in London tried calling my phone now they'd only disturb tope or crab on the sea-bed.

The night is closing on the coast too urgently for the mind to fully contextualise the change of light. There's only the persistent, territorial cry of gulls. The only consistent interpretation of their cries is that they are the true owners of this part of the world. We have our towns and cities, but all this truly belongs to them. I listen to the silence of the cottage, creaks from the ceiling, the winds outside, remembering that I'm still in the dark, that I haven't yet switched on any lights. The peninsula is uneasy with its own silence, with only the sound of gulls, the ever-present gulls. I listen carefully to my conscience and in spite of everything I know something important is taking its course.

The fog-horn is mute, the gap in the life of the peninsula it creates unsettling. Pat Finch must be right – they've muted the fog-horns along the coast. All our lives we've had fog-horns to warn of danger out at sea and now they're gone. So much of what is beautiful is becoming superfluous to the world, replaced incrementally until the vision of the world reflects the view from a wholly different set of eyes.

Since leaving Belgium so many years ago I've controlled my impulses towards women by simple will-power. I avoid the objective view, allowing only the strictest second or two of appreciation of the female form on underground trains and city streets. Through mental discipline I disavowed the obsession of sexual voyeurism. I'd think only of Corinne, her body, words and mind. Since Brussels I've known where an unwanted thought toyed with for a second longer than necessary can lead. I worked at it for year after year, not looking at the pretty faces – not daring to.

In the absence of Corinne thoughts of Jemma Finch are increasingly obscene. I invent scenarios where we savagely couple, her breasts crushing down on me, mothering words caressing the length of me. We writh to a tit-fucking climax and lie together afterwards, depleted, bare chest against her breasts. I'm staggered by this shamelessness; to fantasise like that about another man's wife after all that's passed, to betray the friendship of Pat Finch with thoughts of mammary infidelity. To entertain that kind of weakness again, even without the sanctity of mind, is unforgivable. The self-control perfected over many years means nothing when pushed up against the impact of Jemma Finch on my emotional life. It's useless to try and eject her from my thoughts completely. The fear of another obsession scrambles into position as the dominant fear.

The rotating eye of the lighthouse is blinking out a beam every twenty seconds, a colossus vigilant against the murderous rocks. One man's guilt means nothing here, among Norman bones and Cisterian ruins, a sanctuary for so many malefactors. They'd have powered the light with coal initially, then oil-lamps before the age of electricity, radio beacons in the age of radio. Soon they'll convert them into guesthouses, sign them over to the tourist board. Now and then they'll display the light; beam it out gloriously like the old days. And guests will marvel that mariners actually depended for their lives on an edifice so quaint.

The newspaper clippings from the Karpov-Korchnoi match are useless now that they've yielded their true meaning, that avoidance from another place, another time. It's all so irrelevant, the merciless recollections of a foreign city and a dying father. Under the influence of the lighthouse they've lost their power. The 'Encyclopaedia of Chess Openings' and the chess set are now meaningless too and without sentiment I dump them in the bins around the side of the cottage. There's nothing here to hold me, other than an intensifying fondness for Pat and Jemma Finch. The mercy of the sea is lapping against the shore in forgiveness. The lighthouse can't verbalise words but it speaks volumes of light. It too is forgiving, at worse indifferent to long-ago sins. There's nothing to say that the nausea and dizziness won't return back in London, the pain a sharp barb at the base of the skull. Only the first process is over, the real work yet to come.

Nothing further can be served here. What must happen in London must happen, even if it's a death sentence on the Central line between the morning and evening rush-hours. The only possible direction is Greenford. The sea and the lighthouse have given all they can give, given beyond expectation. Only fate itself can decide the ending.

Chapter 14

Everything is packed and ready to go; what there is to pack. It fits with room to spare into the single piece of wheeled luggage waiting at the cottage door. The coast soaks up the rain, falling solemnly like baptismal water on the converted. The rain revives the earth, teasing to life a hundred subtle smells - a dominant clammy smell like rainwater-rotted timber hanging shroud-like over the edge of land.

I close my eyes momentarily on the short walk to the bungalow, indulging in thoughts of Jemma Finch. But that's only because I know within a matter of hours I'll be leaving. She doesn't know how she touched me, as often women don't know their true effect on men. I bury the kindness of her husband and the attendant guilt in a dormant compartment of the mind, then picture Jemma Finch bathing topless in the swimming cove on the far side of Raven Head. On the sunniest, warmest day of the year she's splashing in the water, diving forward onto a gentle wave that delivers her onto the softness of the sand. I'm alongside her, hyper-energised by her presence. She dries off laughing, facing me, not ashamed of showing the purity and strength of her form. On a beach-towel I massage sun-block into her powerful shoulders and upper back. When she turns over I begin to do her front, our eyes locking. She mouths my first name and it tingles like a warm, moist sponge running the length of my spine. Wordlessly I remove the lower part of her bathing costume.

The violence of a wave erupting on nearby rocks disturbs the fantasy. By the might of the sea beneath the majesty of stars guilt again finds me, gesticulating with more reasons as to why I must reject my own nature. The lights from the windows of Finch's bungalow are torments for those passing who've been cast outside concepts of home. The light from the windows creates an ideal, a paradigm of family and love. It's not the time to fantasise about another man's wife, not the time to even conceive of her as a separate entity outside of her family. But yet in the face of logic, I need to see Jemma Finch as much as I need to see her husband.

The lights from the bungalow are so evocative of home that I see Greenford in them. Beyond the walls I see not into the Finch's home, but into the perfection of our bedroom in the suburbs of London, see Corinne's favourite black and white prints of sun-sets positioned between photographs of our cats when they were kittens on a high shelf. She captured the stages of a cycle trip we made in Dorset with the camera she's had since her last year at university. The grainy prints from the old film-camera are framed in a progressive sequence on one wall. I think about her in Prague when we stumbled on a Jewish cemetery, how she spent hours among the mossy, angled stones, trying to de-cipher family names and dates of final departures. Poised in admiration for her I waited patiently without a word, enduring all the hanging around for the higher ideal of our love.

She snapped roll after roll on the manual thirty-five millimetre with the loud mechanical clicks accompanying each function, lying and kneeling, oblivious to the earth and grass stains accumulating on her jeans. She stooped with the lens focused on an obscure point of relevance important only to her. She needed to suffer somehow, needed to embrace a physical connection with the tragedy of the empty cemetery. At one point she went down on her knees on a patch of tarmac that formed part of a pathway through the graves, that particular shot more evasive than the others. She looked like a penitent from the Catholic Ireland of another time, suffering the pain of kneeling on a hard, gritty surface – offering it up for the abstract and sacred. I waited, patient as the headstones.

That night in the hotel room I noticed scratch-marks on her knees and elbows, the evidence of her determination to connect through her lens with the pain of the holocaust. From the various experiences during those few days in Prague those hours in the cemetery satisfied her the most. Back home in Greenford she took care to arrange the cemetery photos into a special album that she still keeps in our bedroom. In the last few years she's hardly lifted her camera from the cupboard she keeps it in, on top of a stack of jewellery design catalogues I should have tossed out years ago. The interior of the bedroom is part of the permanent furnishings of my mind, everything arranged and scented by her. I miss her breathing by me each night. I miss everything about her, all her imperfections.

At the front door I pause to control a rising and rather frightening expectation, an excitement that touches a part of me that must be ignored. I straighten up, press on the doorbell, try to look normal, or at least liberated from thoughts of self-destruction. Pat Finch quickly opens the door, extending gestures of expansive welcome. His shirt-sleeves are rolled up, slippers on his feet. He'd have dropped whatever he was doing and dashed to the door the second the doorbell sounded. Within seconds I'm aware of a devastating absence, a realisation of emptiness. Jemma Finch is not at home, perhaps busy with a routine family arrangement or taking the kids out for a treat. I think momentarily of the house of her sister's illness, the old Labrador with the flapping teats. I can easily see Jemma Finch in that house, selfless and practical.

Her absence is immediately noticeable, the bungalow interior bereft without her personality dominating all its spaces. Finch directs me to the kitchen, talking about a robbery on the peninsula. They took a racing-motorcycle from the back of a neighbours' house. He's grave and totally humourless as he reports the crime. He wants to know if I've taken all due precaution in the cottage, locking all doors and windows, not leaving valuables lying around. He's shaking his head as he contemplates the question of the stolen motorcycle, couldn't sound more concerned. I didn't think it'd happen here on the peninsula, he says ... not in my lifetime.

The thieves couldn't be from around here.

Just be careful. Don't leave anything lying around.

I'd like to remind him that the only valuable possession I brought with me I lost through my own stupidity, the phone swallowed by the sea. But I'm afraid of sounding self-pitying. It's a big deal for him, crime and robbery on the peninsula. The bits and pieces in the lighthouse-cottage are not worth taking, but then it's not about me. He's reflecting the fears of a man with a wife and young children, a man with valuables. He must have thought about the telescope, how easily it'd fit on the shoulder of an opportunistic thief. He frowns on crime with the expected disgust of a man with no experience of it either way, his conscience merely pricked now and then by omission, a chore left undone.

He'd lose sleep if he'd been too exhausted from a recycling shift to drive off on yet another mission of mercy to his wife's sister. He rummages in a kitchen drawer, mumbling darkly about a perceived decline in the country, an irretrievable disconnection between the lives of ordinary people and collective morality. I remember that fragment of conversation from the pub, the screaming man running through the village at closing-time, mind eaten up by unseen horrors, a picture of knives and drugs. Pat Finch is close to that mid-point in life where a creeping alienation defines more and more of his relationship to the world, where the inevitable mistakes of the young become insufferable. It happened to me around the age he is now; the onset of a process where men grow weary of the world, more conscious of their limitations and morality.

He finds what he's looking for, a dusty bottle of supermarket wine among condiment jars and stacks of cups and saucers. With an ambiguous sigh he positions the bottle and two cut-glass tumblers on the kitchen table where I sit. I'm thirsting for whisky but put the thought of asking him for some out of my mind as he obviously hasn't got any. He's not the kind of man to keep whisky at home. The absence of his wife and girls subtracts from the interior, their lack of presence more emphatic than as if they've just popped out for an hour or two.

He sits heavily on the other side of the table, looking at me as if he's just realised I haven't said much. Any element of silence on the peninsula can instantly provoke vulnerability and vague frowns. It's a local code that people must talk whether or not they're espousing matters close to their hearts or not. Words are a necessary currency of survival around here. We sit uncertainly, sharing an uncomfortable impasse. There's relief on his face when he thinks of something to say.

I don't want to sound like it's the end of the world ... but you must have noticed how things are going.

Sure ... I read the papers.

Where's it all going to end? Where?

My wife believes things are getting better not worse ... an incurable optimist.

He reacts at the mention of her. He can't hide anything; it simply re-arranges his expression for all to read. He's a musical instrument played constantly by the moods and thoughts coursing through him. He's wary, a shift in body language, arms held defensively. He's suspicious, not wishing to cause offence but at the same time unwilling to feed the delusion. I can't help tying to imagine what he sees when he looks at me. How pathetic I must appear in his eyes; womanless and without friends, cast onto the peninsula like an injured mammal by a giant wave. It'd be pointless mentioning Regent Street appointments or jewellery fairs in opulent hotels or the filthy lucre they'd paid me for jewellery designs. It'd mean nothing to him. He wouldn't believe any of it anyhow.

Jemma insists that you'll have to join us for dinner one evening.

She's not here tonight?

She's brought the girls to her mother's place.

They'll be back soon.

I hope he doesn't notice a disquieting dimension in my expression when I mention his wife. I'm astute in these matters, in hiding feelings, but out here the normal expectations are suspended under the influence of the sea. Nothing can be taken as a given. I hope he doesn't notice my eyes brightening at the mention that Jemma Finch is soon due home. There are yet fundamentals in the world, the traumatic effects of women on men. Even here by the sea we're pathetically vulnerable. I'm embarrassed, as if he's glimpsed into a definitive nook of my psyche. I change the subject with unnecessary speed. I'm leaving the peninsula very soon, I say. I must get home to my wife.

As the words leave my lips I see that look on Pat Finch's face again, a look that hangs vulnerably between fear and distress. It's a look that frequently appears when an ambiguous or undefined mien appears in our conversations. When he speaks he sounds far too like a lover trying to smooth out what wasn't meant to be said.

When are you going?

Soon ... probably tonight.

He shouldn't care what happens to me, generally people don't. Why should anyone care out here in the very lap of the sea? It's not like he has a visible gap of need in his life. He's got more than any man can ask for. In a world craving for love, he's cocooned in love.

I'm touched he cares what happens to me, how concern reads so easily on his face.

But you said you wanted to look at the stars.

There may not be time.

It's all very sudden.

He's holding the supermarket wine in the pouring position, frozen into a life-size still by the thoughts playing in his mind. It's of meaning to him, the fact that I'm leaving. There's an absence of indifference in his words. Having seen the relevance of my life reflected for so long in the responses of Corinne it's unsettling to see it in others. The insularity of my life in London makes it harder to understand when others express concern without any apparent condition.

I'm missing my wife ... life doesn't make any sense without her.

He snaps out of his still-life impersonation, tipping cheap wine from the dusty bottle into the glasses on the table between us.

Have you booked a flight?

No ... I thought I might catch the morning ferry to Pembroke. From there I can catch a train or maybe hire a car.

He's almost maternal, eyebrows furrowing in empathy. How the universe has smiled on the Finch girls, suckled in love, brought up to worship the stars, animated by sea-air. I think about the relentless coldness of my own father, his legacy of perpetual damage. Reach for the glass, raise it. We clink glass-edges in salutation. To the future, I say without irony.

After the quickest sip of wine Finch bounces to his feet, surprising in his suddenness. He disappears into the living-room without a word and returns with a cordless phone. He doesn't want to see me queuing at a cold, early-morning ferry-port, roughing it on the Irish Sea. And then a tedious land journey through Wales and into the heartlands of England. I barely taste the wine, trying to sound agreeable.

You don't need to go to any trouble. I'd love to leave by sea.

It's only an hour by air.

If I leave on the morning ferry ... I'll see the lighthouse fading out of view. I can't think of a better way of leaving.

He pauses with the phone in one hand, reaching with his free hand for the wine bottle. His expression, the cordless phone, the cheap supermarket wine are frozen in a triptych of concern. He forgets that he's decades late, that I'm fully grown by now, culpable for my actions in the eyes of the law and my fellows. When I needed him or someone like him there was no one around, in that different time, that room in the Hotel Eugene Plasky; the earlier days in that dark house in our dead town.

It'd be no trouble to arrange a flight.

I'm looking forward to the ferry.

You could wait until tomorrow at least

It's time to go Pat ... I'll stay in touch.

He knows I won't stay in touch, knows that once I step away from the lighthouse-cottage time will rush in to cover my tracks. The minutes and hours will conceal the brief span of my residence here by the sea with the haste of a perpetrator fleeing from an indecent crime. Within days it'll be like I've never set foot here. Yet I say I'll stay in touch, as people say they'll stay in touch: but of course I won't.

The wine tastes more like sweetened vinegar than actual wine, but he's already drained his glass and is pouring a re-fill. I try to imagine him at dinner-parties in London arranged by Peter Branwitz's Regent Street connections, the things he might say and how the others would faultlessly ignore him. If I was staying longer I'd please him with gossip picked up from the jewellery-house banquets Branwitz used to coerce me to attend; tit-bits of intrigue and infidelity, a famous name or two dropped for effect. I'm the guest informant after all, my role to provide the information required.

Finch wants to hear more about the latest development in my plans, probes without his usual circumspection, without troubling to sound unobtrusive. I tell him about the arrangement with the auctioneer, there's a month left to go on the rental contract for the cottage.

And you must have paid him a deposit.

If I give you the keys you can keep the deposit. That's if the auctioneer returns it.

193

Why wouldn't he return it?

I don't know ... people do things like that.

I doubt if Pat Finch is equipped to deal with the fundamental deviousness of the auctioneer, unable to find the right words at the moment the auctioneer points out the cottage's neglect and blames it on a contractual omission or act of maliciousness on my part. The man would instinctively refuse to part with what's due.

I'd be happy to hold the keys. Jemma's sister would love a break on the peninsula but we haven't got the space for them here.

Good, that's settled. You can hold the keys. Do what you wish with the place until the 29th of this month. If he gives you the deposit, please keep it.

If the auctioneer parts with the deposit-money he's holding it'll cover a treat of pony-club lessons for Finch's girls or another attachment for his telescope. I hope he knows it's nothing to what was given. He's already on his third glass of cheap wine, smacking his lips like what he's seen wine-tasters on t.v doing. He hasn't noticed I've hardly touched my glass, or maybe he has noticed but he's too polite to mention it. He's not strong in drink; that was clear from the first occasion in the pub. One can only guess why he's throwing back an inferior concoction from a supermarket shelf. It's hardly his style. I wonder if he's unduly troubled, if Jemma Finch's absence from the bungalow is purely incidental.

Pat Finch is constitutionally unsuited to the whole concept of the domestic dispute. She'd never have to say or do much to push him into a corner. He's miserable. They must have argued – an argument serious enough for her to take the kids to the house of a relative. Naturally he's hiding the hurt and humiliation, pretending to expect her home soon. The fall-out with our respective women draws us closer, a brotherhood of reflection on hasty words or deeds, or the unforgiven sins of the past.

He scrapes his chair back with a jarring screech of timber on floor-tiling, looking downwards intently. Then he straightens up, clears his throat as if he's got something important to say.

We were very worried about you ... we didn't know where it was all heading.

He uses the plural, a distance between the sentiment expressed and his personal feelings. Or else he's hiding the fissures in his home life between a perceived united front. He's sagging in the chair, shoulders dropping, eyes reddening from the vile brew he's swallowed. I'm even more touched by his concern, considering the absence of his wife. He must be worried about her, about the rift or argument they must have had.

That business on the strand, passing out like that ... it's not my style.

We were afraid ... you know, we were worried that you came here for a particular reason. We thought you were making arrangements ...

Arrangements to end my life?

I don't want to sound out of place, but that's what we were thinking.

From the first moments I've arrived here he's watched me from his window, wondering why I'd come alone without a car or with hardly any possessions. He'd have registered the grave expression, that look of fear I brought with me from London. On the first day he'd have mentioned it to his wife, the hunch that their latest neighbour was preparing to wade into a high tide when the conditions were right. From the very first day he initiated his very own coastal suicide watch. I wondered why I was forever bumping into him whenever I stepped from the cottage.

I'm not saying it didn't cross my mind ... but that's not why I came here.

The sea-air ... that's what you said brought you here.

That's right ... the sea-air.

Something must have happened in London.

Sure ... something happened. My wife tried to help, wanted to arrange appointments. You know ... therapy.

But you came here instead.

He saved my life, was quick to hear the shouts from the direction of the rocks. Immediately he abandoned his telescope, rushed to find me prone, close to a night-tide. If I owe any man a debt it's Pat Finch. If there are concepts of natural justice yet relevant he can ask me any question he so chooses. Nothing ought to stand between us, or practically nothing. He pauses, sniffs at his glass, face contorting as if he's only just realised what poison he's been drinking.

You know we have groups here too John ... places where people can go.

For things like that to work ... the patient must have faith in the process.

I thought like that too before I went along. You see it happened to us ... my brother, eleven months younger than ... We were close.

He can't talk about it, lowers his head so that it's almost touching his knees, so that he's almost kneeling forward onto the kitchen floor. He must have felt so helpless, without answers. One can imagine the hurt, what they all went through. He's not raising his head, remaining motionless, incapacitated by emotion.

The telescope Pat ... could I look through it before I go?

That gets through to him instantly, infiltrating the loss of his departed brother and the sadness of whatever separates him from his wife and girls. He straightens up, eyes rheumy, smiling unhappily, apologising. The telescope has saved both of us from the embarrassment of loss. The melancholy of his brother's suicide follows us from the quiet interior to the elevated mount of the telescope. It's a relief to taste the sea-air, the salty bite of night on the peninsula. As if in a grand gesture of salutation the heavens have spread themselves magnificently above the shorelands, more stars visible than what a man could contemplate in a lifetime. Burdened by memories of his brother or perhaps by another sadness he gestures for me to go first, to plunge an eye into the cosmos through the powerful lens. He speaks softly as I step forward, crouching for the optimum view. I seen it in you that first day ... the same look my brother had.

I know what you mean.

It couldn't have been easy for you ... alone at night in the cottage ... no one to talk to.

Something happened once ... a long time ago ... I had to think it through.

That's why you came here?

I guess so.

In a city like London there'd be opportunities, the critical moment when the offer to pay off someone's debt might save their life, or the willingness to listen for as long as it takes. One life, maybe more. But one life at least. The psychic pain of an earlier year brought me here and for once Corinne couldn't help. If anything our conversations in bed made things worse not better. She as good as begged me to sign up for therapy. Naturally I refused, imagining the analyst's face when it got to the point where I had to tell all about what happened to Sonia, the events from Brussels. Hurting her by terminating what remains of my life on the Central line isn't the answer – that's one truth whispered by the sea. By living, a human life is gained. It'll be a challenge, the initiation of conversations with troubled strangers in rail-stations; an observant attendance in hospital waiting-rooms.

My eye is on the lens, light filtering through the iris, adapting to other worlds, scanning the skies for Orion. He's too occupied with his thoughts to enthuse about the telescope. For the first time the stars are peripheral to Pat Finch, nothing but a backdrop to his musings. He's looking downwards as he speaks, almost as if the stars don't exist.

We were brothers ... close all our lives ... but he had his own life. If I'd have known what was going on in his head I'd have taken time off work, looked out for him ... just as I looked out for him when we were kids.

The nebulae and star-clusters dominate the night magnificently. He needs to talk rather than star-gaze, his wife and girls elsewhere, the cheap alcohol reacting against the night-air. He needs to talk, to talk fearlessly to a man he'll never see again. Out of nowhere there's mutual realisations of the power of the night and we're speechless for minutes. Only the stars are relevant enough to unsettle his need to talk. Then he's pointing out the direction of Mars, a pearl of red light above the sea. I step back from the telescope to allow him his turn, but he's disinterested in the view through the lens, only wishing to talk. It's hard on people when things like that happen, he says ... you often wonder what keeps us all going.

Slowly the cosmos is lifting him out of the trough, easing his thought-life above the pain of his brother's death. He straightens up, then at last tilts his head towards the stars. They'd have got him through so much, working his telescope from horizon to horizon, imagining NASA probes infiltrating the carbon-dioxide atmosphere of Mars to search for signs of life, even through there are no evidence of signs of life. Probing on like the mother of a murder victim who refuses to believe there's no hope of ever seeing her child again; glimpsing the dead child in the crowds but when she turns to embrace her finds the face of yet another stranger. What is the measure of this loneliness that drives us to such extremes? On an earlier night by the telescope Finch told me about an Italian astronomer who once identified a series of straight lines criss-crossing the surface of Mars. Then an American by the name of Lowell claimed the lines were evidence of crops irrigated by canals. The world then thought it was a true sign of Martian civilisation, but it was just another sign of mankind's unbearable loneliness. Pat Finch is getting in a mood to again speculate on the majesty of the stars. We tried everything but we never found life out there ... so eventually we put life out there.

I don't follow.

The European Space Agency sent over six hundred forms of life into space to see if they could survive. Most of them didn't ... Only one form of bacteria survived.

We colonised space with bacteria.

That's about it.

Space talk has taken him out of the zone of sadness he's been languishing in since my melancholy reminded him of his brother's fate. He approaches the telescope, eye greedy on the lens, in his shirt-sleeves he's oblivious to the chill of night, as if he's diving physically into the cosmos.

I wonder what his thoughts are on murder, or if he's ever really given it much thought. If I went through it in detail, what happened all those years ago, he wouldn't believe me. He wouldn't alter his expression with even a blink. He'd assume I was talking about a conversation overheard in a pub or a plot from a television drama. If I pressed the point, gripped one of his wrists and stared hard into his eyes he still wouldn't believe it. He'd think I'd been drinking or that the isolation of the peninsula had tipped my reason all to one side. What happened back then is too grotesque to swallow here by the sea and the stars. He's speaking abstractly, like as if he's only addressing himself, eye firmly on the lens.

A kind of worm they scooped up from a pond ... that's what survived the experiment ... proved strong enough to survive the conditions of space ... capable of living in hundreds of degree centigrade ... both plus and minus.

He couldn't comprehend the machinations of a conscience pricked by the death of a woman like Sonia, his mind occupied by the ghosts of NASA probes and creatures from ponds propelled far into space. If he'd ever met Sonia he'd have tried to talk to her about the Andromeda Nebula or the Geminids.

There's a changing mood beneath the stars. Jemma Finch and the girls ought to be here by now and I ought to be on my way. The cosmos is losing its meaning for Pat Finch in the absence of his family. He's worried that she hasn't called by now, excuses himself, says he must make a phone-call. His head is down again as he disengages from the telescope and makes for the side-door of the bungalow. His expression is crowded by the temporary withdrawal of all that has meaning to his

201

heart. I hate having to witness it, what just an apparently minor rift is doing to him.

It's not that late but Corinne's probably already in bed. Teaching does that to her, coloured rings forming under her eyes. Her concentration is often fragmented at meal-time conversations. More than once she's lost it, tiredness sparking off her temper. Like Pat Finch it's not difficult to read her moods. In the last year or two we've spoken more and more about retiring to the French countryside, selling up in Greenford and buying one of those rustic Normandy cottages they like to celebrate in Sunday newspaper supplements. Now, this coastal interlude will dominate the conversation for some time to come.

I stand back from the telescope, taking in the night with the naked eye. When he returns after only a few minutes he's a changed man. He must have gotten through to her, must have smashed whatever was holding them apart from each other. He's grinning, or at least the beginnings of a grin are discernible in the starlight.

They were planning to stay at their granny's house tonight, seeing as there's no school tomorrow. But I just rang Jemma. They're on their way home.

The reminder that it's a weekend night brings a fresh anxiety, the times of ferries probably altered. Finch is gesturing towards the telescope, inviting me to again stoop in front of the lens. I hesitate, as the cosmos have already gifted us enough for one night. We both have things to do, preparations to see to.

I've got to go ... thanks for everything.

You're not staying to say goodbye to Jemma?

It's late ... I'll ring when I get back to London.

As I move towards the side-door of the bungalow it's almost like he's ready to block me physically, to keep me there talking about the stars. Stepping into the interior I know he's close behind. Through the living-space of the interior he's apologising for the lack of decent alcohol, frowning towards the remnants of the vile wine on the kitchen table. Then he gestures helplessly.

The in-laws were around lately. The brother-in-law had what whisky was there.

We pass without comment through the living-space, desolate without Jemma Finch and the girls. At the front door, just before I step back into the night, he almost asks me to stay longer. But by then there's no need for actual words. He knows I have to go, knows that decisions are not merely the consequence of processes within the mind. Even here in the middle of nowhere fate is like a third party present in every conversation and interaction.

Outside the darkness of the night is surprising, as if in the minute or two it's taken for us to walk through the bungalow the light throughout the universe has fundamentally altered. Logically it has to be an illusion to do with the frailty of the human eye and the number of seconds required for the pupils to fully process light. But there's a parallel impression too, to do with the incomplete concept of fate that haunts the past, those events on that hill of rain and tram-lines and in the attic-rooms of the Hotel Eugene Plasky when someone as beautiful as Sonia had to die. Finch is out in the night too, frantically rubbing the palms of his hands together for a reason of his own.

I can drive you to the ferry. It wouldn't be any trouble.

There's no need ... but I'd appreciate it if you rang for a taxi

Sure. When are you leaving?

I'm ready now. I'll wait in the cottage. I'll leave the keys on the window-sill by the front door.

When we shake hands in farewell he uses the same weak handshake as our first meeting. He's a powerful man, hands and fingernails never free from the taint of his work. His palms are calloused and he forever smells of industrial cleaning gel. He's probably worried about crushing my hand, worried about offending me with his strength. Distant car headlights distract him, a vehicle pulling in from the coast road. He's watching the headlights, the progress of the vehicle, as he speaks. I hope you found some answers, he says.

I think I have.

You look better than you did.

I have things to do in London ... a life to save for a start.

The headlights have distracted him, prevented him from hearing the meaning to my words. He's monitoring the vehicle's arrival with the utmost of concentration. It's Jemma Finch and her girls, home late. His world is in place again, the components of his heart stacked neatly into order. I'm gone before the car pulls into the parking-space in front of the bungalow, mindful of the hour of night, knowing that Pat and Jemma Finch have their girls to see to, their own personal complexities to regulate.

I'm gone before he can protest, through the darkness and into the cottage to wait for the taxi to the ferry. I'm cleansed by the sea, conscious of a fresh energy and brighter thoughts, knowing that every breath must be dedicated to Corinne. As I wait the lighthouse looks on mutely, silenced by progress, influencing forever all who pass before it.

CPSIA information can be obtained at www.ICGtesting.com
Printed in the USA
BVOW022355230412

288442BV00002B/1/P